Adventures in Lacacia

Daniel William Krause

This is a Daggerheart-inspired work.

Preliminary editing by Tahnee-Ellen Evans.
Front cover and official editing by Andrew Murphy info@webzvision.com

Acknowledments

How many of these have you read, where the author thanks a person or people for being there or inspiring them? I would assume many. Well, it's my turn. So many people in my life have come and gone, but there are definitely five who will always remain constant. To my beautiful and amazing, crazy children.

Phoenix, Lincoln, Matilda, River and Baden.

No matter what happens and others tell you, I love you, always.

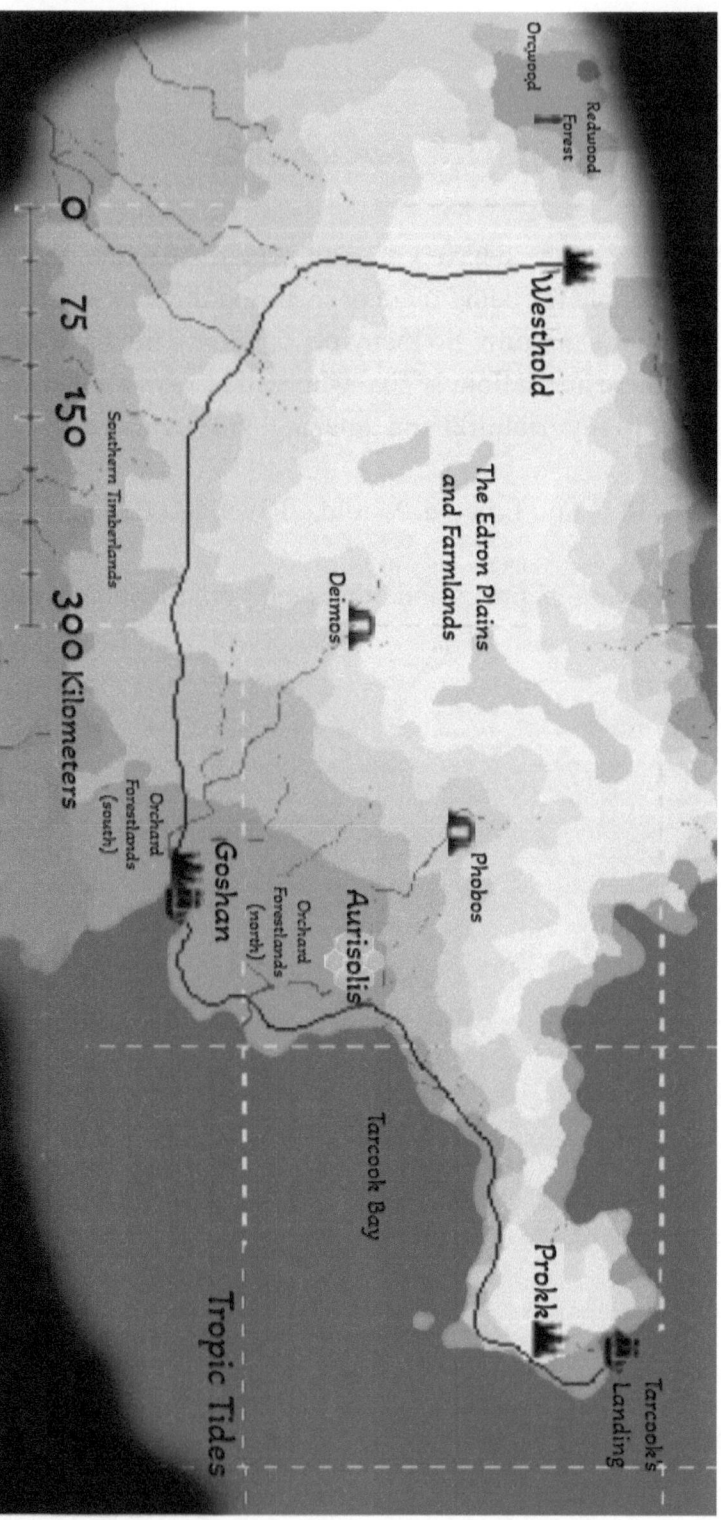

Chapter One

The street was alive with the bustling of citizens in the heart of commerce. The early morning sun had lifted high enough over the city's buildings to light up the marketplace. Looming graciously on the square's east side was the Great Keep, home of the Lord Governor of Goshan.

Goshan was home to many people of different races. The most common were Dwarves, Elves, Halflings and Humans. However, that was not all: other races included Drakona, Faeries, Goblins and Ribbets. Goshan was a major city on the coast of a region called Edron. Not so much a country or a state, but an area of land that is governed by Lord Governors, from the three largest cities in Edron: Goshan, Prokk and Westhold.

The architecture of the city incorporated tuden style dwellings with blue tiled roofs, some with stone foundations. Larger structures, such as towers and the Great Keep, were made completely of stone and painted in two-tone, white and a light sea blue colour. Just outside the city, located right on the shore, was the port of Goshan, a hub of shipping and trade under the authority of the Terrapin Syndicate. Here on the docks, another race of people is found, the Galapa. Human-sized turtle folk that spend most of their time on the sea, where they feel at home the most.

Goshan and the other cities in Edron were not heavily fortified settlements. There are a few sentry towers on the outskirts, but since the region is at peace, a strong military force was not required. A small contingent of city guards was employed by the Lord Governor to maintain public order within the communities.

As the citizens went about their daily business, shopping for food and items, and enjoying a hot brew at one of the cafes, a small group of city guards began to round the corner and enter the main market square. Six guards were positioned, three per side, of an armoured carriage making its way through the crowd. A seventh guard, the commanding officer, was out in front speaking in a loud, firm voice.

"Make way, please, coming through. Make way."

The crowd hears this and responds in turn, moving aside to let the carriage pass through the main street.

While this was happening, on the south side of the market square, a group of minstrels were setting up a stage and instruments. They are being supervised by a male Halfling, with lightly tanned, caucasian skin and short, curly red hair, wearing some of the finest attire that money can buy. Nearby was a seven-foot Apis-fae, just hovering above the stone street, cautiously watching, not to interfere with the carriage as he samples some honey and nectar from a local vendor. Across the way, a blue and pink Ribbet was making its way through the market, pursuing the wares of a clothing stall and finally, a sight that has never been seen before: a large mushroom-shaped individual, with arms and legs, the colour of white ash and carrying a wooden staff. As it aimlessly wanders through the crowd, looking in every direction, the rest of the crowd stared in awe at this creature. The Halfling, while supervising his work crew, momentarily looked at the carriage as it rounded the corner and noticed a suspicious individual, in a dark cloak, lurking nearby.

KABOOM!

A loud, exploding noise erupts, and smoke instantly begins to pour out from under the carriage, filling the vicinity. The carriage itself stopped dead in the street, as one of the rear wheels came loose and rolled across the square, the axle hitting the ground and grinding in the stone. The guards and some of the nearby citizens began to cough and choke, as they keel over. The lead guard, still affected by the smoke, managed to look up and over at the Halfling and the Apis-fae and yelled.

"Stop them, that item is extremely valuable!" as he pointed in the direction of the thief, still bent over, coughing.

At the same time, the Ribbet and the mushroom person saw this and decided to lend a hand. The mushroom person fired a stream of arcane energy across the square, and before the thief had a chance to make their timely escape, they were pushed across the street and into a market stall. As instantly as the thief was pushed, vines began to sprout up out of the stone street and entangle the thief, restricting their ability to move. The Ribbet moved forward, closing the gap between them and the thief. Without warning, the thief managed to unsheathe a serrated blade and made a swipe at the Ribbet, and was cut with it, leaving an extensive gash.

Now, the Halfling and the Apis-fae had made chase and entered the fray, just as the mushroom person lifted and pointed its staff and, from its end, shot a stream of fire at the assailant. Still entangled in the vines, with no way to escape, the thief began to burn and eventually dropped to the ground in silence. As they all looked up from the body lying still on the ground, they noticed that the nearby stall had also caught fire.

"WATER, WATER, WE NEED WATER OVER!" The Halfling yelled. The onlookers, now in a panic, hurriedly moved about. The stallholder jumped to the side away from the flames.

The Ribbet moved forward and cast a spell; a gust of wind flowed out in an attempt to extinguish the fire, but it only caused the fire to spread more. The Apis-fae, who went looking for a water source, returned with buckets of water in each of their four hands. He passed them to the mushroom person and the Halfling as they worked together to bring the fire under control. Luckily, the fire had not become too large, and the few pails were enough to extinguish the flames, saving the majority of the stall.

By now, the commotion was dying down, and several more guards had entered the market square to provide assistance. The smoke had cleared away from the armoured carriage, and the lead guard who had spoken before had regained his composure.

The four individuals who had dispatched the would-be thief searched her remains and recovered the item taken from the carriage. It was surprisingly undamaged from the flames. A large one-foot-tall, cylindrical crystal, currently in the soft, fungal hand of the mushroom person.

They approached the lead guard with it and handed it to him.

"I sincerely thank you for your timely actions in 'apprehending' the culprit," he emphasised the word "apprehending" as he looked at the remains of the thief and signalled his fellow guards to remove them from the street.

"You'd be glad to know that the thief didn't seem to be associated with any particular organisation, nor did she seem to be working with anyone else." The Halfling explained.

"She?" The head guard was surprised and also acknowledged the Halflings' meaning of the criminal underground.

"Well, I feel like it is my duty to commend you on a job well done. If you would so please, I would like to bring you before the Lord Governor and inform him of your deeds."

The four individuals all looked at each other for a moment to ascertain their desires and turned to the guard, "We would be delighted."

After ensuring the safety of the public and clearing the marketplace, the lead guard took the four citizens to the Great Keep. As he did, he officially introduced himself as Captain Samuel Tombo, a middle-aged Human male of average height and build, with short, greying brown hair in the back and sides. His attire consisted of a blue gambeson armoured top and a pair of brown trousers, and dark brown leather boots and carried a longsword by his side. A metal insignia of his rank on his left shoulder.

Whilst walking, the four introduced themselves to one another. The Halfling initiated the conversation as if introducing himself onstage.

"I am Purvan Lova, musical extraordinaire, teller of tall tales, student of life and if I may say so, exceptional pleaser of the ladies."

The others looked at him momentarily with a slight awkwardness.

"Well, if we are introducing ourselves, my name is Nectarion Seraphix, and I come from Aurisolis, the kingdom of the Apis-fae, north of Goshan."

A moment passed, and the Ribbet continued the conversation.

"My name is Oophaga Pumilio. I am a wielder of natural magics, taught to me by my tribe."

"Fascinating, and where is your tribe located?" Purvan queried.

"In the north," they responded, remaining somewhat guarded.

The three then turn to the mushroom person, expecting an answer.

"Oh, my turn now, yes. Well, greetings, my name is Pluteus Cyanopus, and I am currently exploring the world, which I have never actually seen before. All this is so amazing. I mean, I have seen things in books, but never have I imagined such amazing sights."

"That is fantastic, my friend, but I would like to know a little more, for example, what are you exactly?"

Nectarion and Oophaga gave a disapproving look toward Purvan for his bluntness, although they too were curious.

"I am a Fungril, a race of sentient fungal people," he explained.

The captain looked over his shoulder at the group with a slight look of exasperation.

Captain Tombo continued to lead the group through the market district of the city, where they eventually approached a ten-foot stone wall, painted a deep sea blue. A massive stone archway granted entrance. Atop, a causeway with guards looking down, and every fifty meters, built into the wall is a sentry tower.

Walking through the archway, Captain Tombo acknowledged the guards and continued down the main stone path through illustrious gardens and parklands. The group noticed the Magic Academy, the Hall of Fire and Mirrors, off to the right.

"*Oooo*, what is that place?" Pluteus asked in awe, "What is a Hall of Fire and Mirrors?"

"That, my fungal friend, is the magic academy. Those with the arcane spark attend the school to train and hone their skills with magic to develop and find ways to better society. The most skilled and powerful form an exclusive order, known as the Novum Arcanum, and serve the Lord Governor." Purvan excitedly explained to him. Pluteus was stunningly mesmerised.

The group reached the main building of the Lord Governor, The Great Keep, and before them stood two large, sturdy and thick wooden doors, hinged with thick iron. Samuel gave three big knocks with the knocker of one of the large doors, and after a brief pause, the doors opened. They entered the large hall of the keep. A beautiful blue carpet lined the floor in the centre of the hall. Large, thick, filigree, wooden columns lined each side of the blue stone hall, about twenty feet apart, and between each were large marble desks, each with an individual seated there, busily working, completing paperwork and completing documents. The 'clomp' of approval stamps hitting the desk is mixed with the scribbles of quills writing on paper.

Continuing further, walking past the clerks, slight glances peered up at the group. Reaching the end of the main hall, the blue carpet continued up a flight of stone stairs with wooden filigree banisters, one of two that occupy each side of this end of the hall. The captain led the group up the first few stairs, which came to a landing that then split towards the left and right. At the top of the landing is a giant window, clear glass framed by coloured stained glass, the morning light projecting colours across parts of the main hall. The view from the window showed the marketplace in the distance, the residential district and then the port and ocean beyond.

The group finally made its way to the first floor, much like the ground floor, which contained only the desk of the Lord Governor, placed at the far end of this hall, with another great window pane behind him. Eight royal guards line the walls, two close to the Lord Governor. Some are Elves, others are Human. The Lord Governor is seated in a chair that resembles a throne, made of timber with an exquisite carved filigree design and inlaid with gold and silver.

Samuel brought the four before him. The Lord Governor noticed their approach and stood to receive them.

The Lord Governor, a male Human named Obo Wolbodo, was an elderly man with short, balding, grey hair, a plump, round midsection and wore two-tone blue robes of office. He wore a reddish leather belt with a golden buckle around the waist and a simple gold circlet crown on his head, signifying his office.

Samuel stepped forward.

"My liege, I bring before you citizens that are of great calibre. They just now assisted my men and I in the recovery of the item we were transporting, as it had been illegally taken from us."

Governor Obo stepped from behind his desk and moved closer to the captain, a look of disdain upon his face.

"Samuel, I would say that is wonderful news, with the exception that it was meant to be well protected, you know the importance of the item, and you have not yet left the city limits"

"I understand, my lord, and I apologise for my negligence in my duty, but with the crisis diverted, all is well?" his last few words were a question, rather than a statement.

"While the item was recovered, all is not well. If you and your men can not exit the city without incident, then it would be assumed that you are unfit for this task."

Samuel's face hardened as he was somewhat insulted. The Lord Governor looked sternly at the captain and then turned to look at the four individuals standing close behind him.

"But it seems that you rectified the issue by presenting me with an alternative."

Samuel looked slightly confused and confounded as the governor looked to the party.

"It seems that your heroics have given you the opportunity to serve your people. I present to you a mission of the utmost importance. An item of great magical significance needs to be transported and delivered to an individual who is an ally of this office."

Purvan stepped forward, reluctantly.

"It is a pleasure to be within your service again, my Lord, but may I ask as to the particulars of this mission?"

The Lord Governor smiled at the presence of Purvan, "Ah, my old friend, please excuse my rudeness, I did not see you there. I am not surprised that you are part of this scenario; you are always looking for a way to make yourself known."

A smirk appeared on Purvan's face.

"The item in question, the crystal, must reach its destination. It must be protected at all costs. It is an extremely powerful, magical item. It needs to be delivered to a sage near Westhold. She is an ally of the Lord Governors and lives in a tower in the Redwood Forest. Once it is in her possession, she will know how to proceed, and then you can return to Goshan."

The group looked at each other curiously, trying to ascertain each other's thoughts, all while the Lord Governor continued.

"I will pay you one bag of gold each for now, and once you have returned with proof that you have completed your mission, an additional bag of gold, courtesy of Captain Samuel."

A look of disappointment fell across Samuel's face as he became aware of the cost of his failure.

The Lord Governor looked intently as the group quietly discussed the request among themselves.

"As the somewhat appointed spokesman of the newly established adventuring party, I am glad to say, we accept," Purvan announced loud and proud.

"Good," the Lord Governor replied with a smile from ear to ear. "Samuel, make the arrangements, please, and no armoured cart this time. Choose something inconspicuous."

Samuel led the party out of the Keep, and as he did, the Lord Governor beckoned to Nectarion to remain a moment.

"I recognise your station, good sir; you served the queen of Aurisolis directly. I am sorry for your loss."

"Thank you, my Lord, your sympathy is greatly welcome," Nectarion replied with the sound of grief in his voice.

"I believe her daughter now sits on the throne?"

"Yes, my Lord."

"If you happen to make your way back home, inform your new queen that if she requires aid, Goshan would gratefully assist. Both our societies rely heavily on each other to survive. Without your people, the Orchard Forests will not be able to produce the yields it does, and our people, all our people, could find themselves in the middle of a food shortage or even famine"

Nectarion bowed to the Lord Governor with reverence, "Thank you, my Lord, I will ensure that my queen will receive the message."

The Lord Governor bade him farewell, and Nectarion left to join his new companions.

Nectarion finally caught up with his newfound friends and, using the down payment of a bag of gold each, they spent a few hours shopping for a few supplies.

While the Ribbet and the Fungril have no essence of the value of coin, Purvan and Nectarion educated them as best they could.

"A bag of gold is actually quite a decent amount of coin," Purvan explained. "If you shop around and look for the deals, you could buy a second-hand cart for half a bag of gold. Not that I have to worry about wealth, I have a nice apartment uptown and Lord Obo and I go way back. He even personally requests that I perform at state parties and diplomatic functions."

As they were shopping, Purvan and Nectarion entered a general store. Here, Purvan bought some seemingly mundane items. A premium bedroll, a woven net, manacles, a suspended rod and a companion case. While Nectarion seemed not to notice, the store clerk gave Purvan a look of suspicious deviation. Purvan placed the gold on the counter and gave the clerk a wink before collecting his purchase and exiting with Nectarion.

The party returned to the archway entrance of the keep, where they were met again by Captain Samuel, who appeared depressed.

"Here you go, this is a pack with some basic supplies and health potions in case you get into a spot of trouble. You will also have this pack mule to help carry any of your packs and supplies should you need." Oophaga took the mule lead from the Captain and began to become acquainted with the animal. There was an instant rapport between the two.

Pluteus was teeming with excitement as he was about to embark on what the others called adventuring, and he was just ecstatic to have met his new compatriots.

Finally, Samuel walked over to Purvan and handed him a small black felt bag with a drawstring.

"What's this?" Purvan asked.

"This is a Bag of Infinite. It opens up, and what you place inside goes into a pocket dimension for safekeeping. These are rare, and they are donated by the Novum Arcanum. The Lord Governor has allowed you to retain this after the mission."

Purvan looked at the bag in comparison to the size of the crystal and noticed that the bag was relatively smaller, but sure as, Samuel opened the bag and placed the large crystal inside.

"This is the so-called inconspicuous means of transport," he remarked. "I am not happy that this task was redirected to you, but I am grateful that you prevented it from falling into the wrong hands. I wish you all the best on your journey."

The captain placed a hand on the Halfling's shoulder in silent well-wishing, then stepped back as they began to depart. It was early afternoon, and there were still a few hours of daylight. The party began their trek, first through the city streets, then the outskirts, passing through the residences and finally out onto the Silverleaf road, heading west.

After travelling for nearly two weeks along the Silverleaf road, past the Southern Timberlands, and then turning north towards Westhold, the party had spent a good deal of time together and had become accustomed to each other's presence. To the west of them is the Redwood Forest, a dense forest of redwood trees and a well-known haven for Orc raiding parties to hide and take advantage of travellers passing by.

With only a few days' travel left, the Redwood became slightly ominous, and Oophaga, whom the party had discovered is a druid attuned to nature, sensed a disturbance in the natural order of the woods. As they continued along the Silverleaf road, the sun began to settle behind the trees of the western forest, and Oophaga detected movement in the trees.

In an instant, three large wolves pounced from the tree line and held up the party. The wolves steadied themselves, ready to deal with any threat that might approach. The party mimic their stance, the two groups at a stand-off, just waiting for the other to make a move.

The three wolves are positioned in a triangular pattern. The lead wolf, bigger than the other two, with greyish-black fur and yellow eyes, stared down at the party. The other two, standing just behind their leader, with a more brownish-black coat, teeth bared, wait for the moment.

Oophaga stared back at the wolves; they motioned to the others.

"Hold your ground, don't make a move unless I say."

"Are you sure?" Pluteus inquired.

Without speaking, the small frog-like druid gestured again for the others to remain calm. They moved gingerly towards the wolves, placed out their hand and lowered their head ever so slightly. The lead wolf turned its head to its pack, as if to gesture 'hold', and it moved cautiously towards Oophaga. Inch by inch, the two drew closer to one another until Oophaga's hand touched the snout of the wolf. A moment passed, then everyone watched as the wolves stood down from their threatening pose.

"Wow, that was amazing. How did you do that?" Pluteus eagerly asked.

They responded, "You use arcane magic, what you read in your books. Druids learn how to wield the magic of nature, given to us by the Nurturing Maiden."

"The Nurturing Maiden, who is that?" asked Nectarion.

"She is a goddess of old, the knowledge of her existence and the magic we use has been passed down for generations, long before the First Age. She is the patron of all druids."

18

Another moment passed as the party pondered the words spoken by Oophaga, and then they all turned to the wolves. Oophaga then explained,

"These are not just normal wolves; these are dire wolves, hence their size, quite rare. They mean us no harm; something has spooked them and driven them out of their territory. They would not be so easily seen outside their protected space."

Pluteus asked, "What should we do?"

Oophaga closed their large, black frog eyes for a moment.

"They say there is a menace that resides in the forest, it has driven them from their home, but it continues to consume. They are helpless."

"These woods are known for Orc raiding parties; it's quite possible that is the menace to which they refer." Purvan speculated to the party.

The dire wolves stared at them for a moment and looked back at Oophaga before they turned and retreated back into the woods.

"Where are they going?" Nectarion asked.

"Back into the woods, they can't stay out here; they would be more exposed"

The wolves entered the forest, and the leader took one more look back at the party before disappearing into the darkness of the trees.

The next day, as the party continued on the road, they noticed, off in the distance to the right of the Silverleaf road, a farmstead. As they drew nearer, they noticed there was quite a stillness about the farm and the lack of sound that a home like this would generate. The party decided to investigate and discovered that the house is empty and dark. There were no signs of people, nor any indication that they had been injured. The furniture was turned over and smashed, and the barn outside had been raided, and the livestock slaughtered.

Pluteus noticed a crop of mushrooms growing just under the main house and, using his ability to communicate with them, he was able to gather some information and share it with his comrades.

"My friends tell me that a few days ago, this farm was raided by the ones you call Orcs, who came from the forest. They didn't see everything, but they believe that the farmers made it out unharmed before the Orcs messed up the place."

With no further clues or information, the party began to continue their journey back out onto the Silverleaf road, ever more cautious about the forest on their left.

After a few more days, the party reached a fork in the road. The Silverleaf road continued north to Westhold for another 25 kilometres, while the signpost also pointed west towards the Redwood Forest, saying 40 kilometres. A dirt track led off the Silverleaf road in that direction. As they approached the sign, Pluteus's staff began to vibrate with an arcane energy and on the signpost, a glyph of some sort appeared, glowing. The party remembered that the Lord Governor mentioned that *'the'* arcane mark will lead the way.

With that, the party headed down the dirt track towards the Redwood Forest.

Chapter Two

The party had been travelling for a few days since they entered the Redwood Forest and had started to become a little complacent. They had begun to believe that they had been sent on a wild goose chase. Walking along the forest road, a dirt track, they rounded the bend and found that trees started to thin out slightly, until they dropped away to reveal a grassy opening in the forest.

The trees of the forest formed a circle around the grassy grove, and in the centre, about six stories high, stood a stone tower with a pointed roof of reddish-brown tiles. Vines grew up the side, and mossy patches filled the gaps between the stone blocks that made up this tower. A standard wooden door framed in stone bricks sat at the base, upon it a simple ornamental knocker. The grass around the base grew taller than the rest of the grove. A few open windows were set in the top half of the tower; the lower half only contained stone blocks.

"I guess we found the goose," Purvan exclaimed. The party just stood there and stared.

"Shall we?" Nectarion suggested as he gestured to the tower and hovered towards it with a buzz.

The party approached the door, and as they reached the front step, the same arcane sigil that had appeared on the road sign appeared on the door, and the knocker magically knocked on it.

A few moments passed, and then the noise of a door bolt being used, and the door swung open. There stood a Halfling woman. Standing only four feet tall, the middle-aged woman, with long, matted black hair that reached down to her mid-back, gave them a dubious look. She wore a simple tunic and trousers with an open mage's robe coloured like dirty puce, used like a bathrobe and upon her feet, fluffy slippers that looked like they were once a small animal's fur.

She stared at the party and then at the arcane sigil, and then back at the party with a wide grin, mouth full of yellowed teeth and build-up between.

"What business do you bring?" the Halfling shouted up at the party with a pitched, raspy voice.

"We have been charged with an important mission to deliver this most precious, magical item," Nectarion announced, and Purvan retrieved the crystal from the magical bag where it had been stored. She stared at the crystal and turned back towards her abode.

"I see, well, enter, enter. Come, come." She simply began to walk away, leading the party across the ground floor to a spiral staircase that ascended upwards.

The party made their way up the staircase inside, ascending what would be two stories before they began passing open doorways,

A kitchen with a small table and one dining chair, a few dirty dishes in a wash tub and the smell of day-old food.

A room full of boxes and books stacked vertically, collecting dust.

Eventually, they reached what would be the fifth floor, which contained the Halfling's study. A few armchairs, old and battered, occupied the room, and a small black pot-belly stove with the chimney that protruded out the window, smoke slowly drifting into the sky. One bookshelf full of books, a small desk, and stool. There is a quill, ink and a few pieces of parchment spread across the desk top.

But the one thing the party noticed before all that is the smell in here and the number of felines sitting or lounging on the armchairs, the bookshelf, the floor, her desk stool, and her desk. There seemed to be at least twenty cats in here.

"Don't mind them," as she shooed away some of the cats and moved to sit in the armchair closest to the window. The oldest and most worn armchair is near her desk. The smell of mould and mildew oozed from it. She beckoned the party to sit.

"I spose I should introduce myself. I am Stellda Furfoot. I know you have been sent by the people in charge of your cities. Who is it now, Hobo?" she queried at the name of the Lord Governor.

"Lord Governor Obo." Nectarion awkwardly corrected her.

"Errr, yes, well, I would not have let you enter if the arcane sigil hadn't activated. Can't be too careful who ya' let in." A moment passed, and she offered, "Do you want some tea?"

The party watched as the pot on the stove magically levitated through the air to meet the cups and saucers.

"You want milk with that?" she asked, and the party looked at where she indicated and noticed two of the cats drinking from the small jug of milk.

Both Purvan and Nectarion declined the offer of milk but accepted the tea. Oophaga happily accepted the milk tea as they patted one of the cats, and Pluteus showed no interest at all.

Now holding and studying the crystal, Stellda examined it closely.

"Err, yes, I see."

"There was a note that came with it that can only be read by arcane means." Purvan handed her the parchment as he explained.

"Err, very well. It will take me a few days to conduct my studies before the job is complete. You can be on your way if you like," she said as she retrieved some parchment from her desk and marked it, handing the note to the party with her arcane seal on it.

"This will be the proof you need for your Lord Hobo," she said as she returned to her seat. "Alternatively, you could stay a few days and deliver it to the mages in Westhold for me."

The party looked at each other for an answer, debating if it would be a good idea to stay here in this place.

"If you do, I will ensure that you are paid another half bag o'gold each," she enticed them, a cheeky grin appearing on her face.

With the promise of a few more coins, the party decided to spend a few days at the tower. It didn't take long for a bard's reputation for saucy scenarios to kick in. As the evening took hold and the others bedded down for the night, Purvan made his way up the spiral staircase to the top floor, Stellda's private quarters. The door is slightly open, and the strong smell of feline perfume hits Purvan's nose. He rattled his knuckles on the door ever so lightly.

Startled, Stellda looked up and saw Purvan as he gingerly and seductively opened the door further to show his presence.

"You startled me," she exclaimed.

"I can't help but have noticed earlier, the look in your eye when we first met," he said smoothly as he entered her chamber. A small cheeky grin showed on her face. A cool breeze flowed into the room, ruffling Purvan's soft, white cotton shirt under his fine blue leather waistcoat. He flicked back his head as if to shift his hair away from his eyes to see Stellda clearly in the dim light of her candlelit bedroom. His crotch thrust forward to emphasise its presence.

She turned to him properly now, "Young man, whatever glint you may have seen was but an arcane spark that flows through my veins. As a sorcerer, we are born with magic in our blood." She worked to rebut his advances, but he moved a little closer. His smooth, calming voice echoed slightly in the chamber.

"Perhaps it was a simple mistake, or perhaps it was a spark. The spark of romance, of love."

Stellda stood now in close quarters with her Halfling counterpart, goosebumps rose upon her skin under her mage robe, and she trembled ever so slightly.

Stumbling over her words, "Do you know…. do you know…. I mean…. I'm."

"Yes, my dear?"

"I am much older than you probably realise," she managed to convey to him.

"Love cares not for age, my sweet, only passion."

Purvan and Stellda lay on her bed, naked in the cool breeze of the early morning hours. They had spent many hours in the heat of passion and physical pleasure, and now they were simply enjoying each other's company.

"I haven't felt anything like that in over two hundred years," she exclaimed with joyous reverence, her body now at ease from the vigorous activities.

"Over two hundred?" Purvan inquired about her statement.

"Yes, my dear, I did try to explain to you, but your immensely smooth charm had me almost collapse to the floor, and then we were…" She trailed off the last of her sentence.

Purvan looked at her with a slight sense of apprehension, but it quickly faded to a cheeky smirk of lust for the old timer.

"So exactly how old are you?"

"Almost three hundred years old."

"You don't look a day over seventy-five." Purvan flattered her.

"It's part of what I do here, my charge, my job. It extends our life by double, sometimes more. My predecessor died at the age of five hundred and eleven, and he was Human."

Purvan was impressed and surprised at the same time. He momentarily looked at her body up and down. She had definitely adapted to the solitary life. Her legs had more hair than a fox's fur coat, her beaver could have been mistaken for an actual beaver, and her pits could be combed. The ensemble was completed with her yellow teeth and her long, black, matted hair. And yet, there was a spark in her eye that Purvan had never seen in any of his conquests before. She appealed to him, the wonders and mysteries she must have seen in her three hundred years.

With a few moments of silence between the two, Purvan broke it.

"So what is the story with the crystal we bought with us? What is so important and magical about it?"

26

She looked at him with a pause of caution, which faded with a look of trust.

"Well, I suppose I can trust you. We have just slept together, so we are betrothed now."

Purvan's face turned to shock, and she cheekily smiled at him.

"The crystal is known as an Omega Crystal. They are very rare, so rare that this is the only known one."

Composure returned. Purvan asked, "So what is an Omega Crystal?"

"It has not been entirely classified. The Novum Arcanum discovered this one at the ruins on the plains of Edron centuries ago. Every hundred years, each chapter gains possession of it and studies it until they can understand it. They also use it to power magical items, including airships."

"So what, it's been a hundred years, and now it's Westhold's turn?" He asked her.

"Yes, but there is more. The mages in Goshan have finally discovered how to create clones of the crystal and transfer the power of the prime crystal to them, allowing for the creation of multiple power supplies."

"Amazing." Purvan listened intently as Stellda explained the process. "Won't the 'prime' crystal eventually run out of power?"

"That's the incredible thing about Omega Crystals: they have an endless supply of power. They are forever regenerating. That is what the arcane note explains, it is only meant for the mages to decipher, to ensure security"

Purvan's face went slightly blank as he processed the information he had just heard. Stellda looked at him in return with concern. A smile returned to his face as he scooped her into his arms.

"Shall we go another round?"

"Okay, but I get to be on top."

The party spent the majority of the day relaxing and enjoying the serenity of the grove. Pluteus remained inside and read through Stellda's library. Oophaga and Nectarion spent their time outside in nature. Purvan woke about midday, looked to his side and saw Stellda soundly sleeping. He rose, dressed, and proceeded down the stairs to mingle with his companions.

He grabbed some food from the kitchen and then found himself with his sleeves rolled up and cleaning. The dishes are done, dried and put away; the rubbish is disposed of; the cats fed; and the table and chairs straightened, with a new tablecloth laid out featuring images of tomes and cats across it. He then continued downstairs and exited the tower to enjoy what was left of the afternoon.

Outside, he saw his friends mulling about the grove and taking in the forest that surrounds the grove. The sun was slowly descending in the west behind the trees of the forest, and the light of the sky dimmed. As the party walked towards the tower door, Oophaga halted their movement. They turned back to look at the forest, something lurking, perhaps their dire wolf friends had come to visit.

"GLARGH!!"

A large, dirty, green-looking creature made a weird, loud cry as it sprang from the tree line and ran directly at the party. As it did, several more emerged behind it. Two more that looked the same as the first attacker, all wielding swords. Another large, more brutish one with no weapon, and at the rear, the final one, brandishing a battleaxe, gripped tightly in both his hands. His stature and attire suggested he is the leader.

The three swordsmen made their way towards the tower and the party. In an instant, Nectarion fired a bolt of arcane energy at the oncoming attackers. He then threw his Hallowed axe at the assailants, but they managed to avoid the weapon. It stopped in mid-air and then began to reverse back to Nectarion, where he held it firmly in his grip with two of his hands.

From out of the fifth-floor window, Stellda appeared, "Oh no, not again. Bloody Orcs, get off my lawn!" Then, looking at the party, "Well, okay, you lot, why don't you make yourselves useful?!"

"I see the menu has meat on it!" Purvan yelled, and an arcane wave washed over the party as they rallied together to attack.

Pluteus stepped forward first and thrust his hands towards the Orcs. A large ice spike appeared from his palms and travelled directly at the enemy. As the ice spike made contact, they were instantly frozen.

Oophaga began to run at the Orcs and shifted their form into that of a wolf. They pounced at the Orcs, grabbing a leg of the brutish Orc in their vice-like jaw. The Orc began to react by trying to shove them off his leg.

From out of the trees, a woosh cut through the air and hit the large, brustish Orc in the torso. He faltered slightly and steadied his stance, his leg still in Oophaga's grip. As the party turned to see where it originated from, a tall, dark skinned individual appeared from the treeline and nocked another arrow, ready, aiming it at the Orcs. The party, unsure of how to react, continued to deal with the Orcs.

Pluteus thrust his hands forward again; another ice spike moved through the air and hit its mark. The three swordsmen fell to the ground, motionless.

Purvan, standing behind his companions, stopped momentarily, and a magical melody emanated from the Halfling.

> *"There once was a person quite frail,*
> *Whose strength was quite hard to prevail.*
> *He'd get blown by the breeze,*
> *And fall down on his knees,*
> *Just trying to walk on a pail."*

As the party heard this, they witnessed the commander stumble a little, and Purvan looked on with a cheeky grin.

Nectarion stepped up now, closer to the brutish Orc and swung his axe at him, bringing him down. He then continued to swing his axe back the other way towards the commander.

Finally, another arrow from the mystery person is loosed towards the commander. It moved through the air and found its mark as it pierced the soft spot between the commander's eyes and exited the back of his head. He stood there for a moment before his body keeled over and hit the ground face-first, arrow still embedded in his cranium.

The party stood there in a state of stupor, looking at their now deceased attackers. Gingerly, the dark-skinned stranger made her way towards them.

"Are you all okay?" she asked.

The party, startled, looked up at the stranger with poise.

"Explain yourself, who are you?" Oophaga inquired with a commanding voice.

From behind the group, the tower door opened, and Stellda peered out cautiously, wand in hand.

"Are they gone?" she asked. Looking at the scene before her, she noticed the party in an aggressive stance towards the stranger.

"NO, WAIT! She's an ally," and she ran over to them all. "Everyone, calm down." She looked at the party and explained. "This is an associate of mine, we are well known to each other. May I introduce Nushala?"

The party relaxed and moved its stance to a passive state. The dark-skinned Elf, with straight blonde hair done up in a bun with twigs and vines, wearing a light green tunic over leather armour and brown trousers with short, soft leather boots, stood confidently before the party. She looked down at Stellda.

"That one was a close one, Shala," the Halfling sorcerer stated to her Elvish friend. "Perhaps you are losing your touch."

"I doubt it." Nushala snickered. She looked at the party and sarcastically remarked, "What is this, are you thinking of replacing me?"

"Pfft, don't worry about this lot, they are just making a delivery and just happen to be of an additional service."

The party looked at each other, disgruntled at the candour of Stellda's comment. She then led Nushala toward the tower and left the party behind.

After a short while, the party ascended the tower and joined Stellda and the ranger, Nushala, in the study.

"Ahh, decided to join us finally?" Stellda candidly remarked.

The party, looking somewhat tired as they had just taken care of the five bodies that littered the grove outside.

"If you must know, we took the Orcs back into the forest for the animals to deal with," Oophaga replied.

"We also checked to see if they had any valuables on their persons." Nectarion continued.

"Oh, fascinating, did you find anything interesting?" Stellda asked.

"Some gold, their weapons and what appears to be a malfunctioning compass," Purvan informed her.

Stellda stood up, moved to Purvan and gestured to inspect the item. She looked it over, waved her hand across it with a slight arcane spark and simply responded,

"Well, I'm sure all will be revealed eventually," she said, handing it back and returning to her armchair, continuing to address the party.

"Nushala and I have been discussing the situation regarding the Orcs. They have gotten too bold for their own good, and it has started to upset the balance of the forest. Shala and I have lived here for some time now. Shala is a guardian of the forest, and I assist her with any supplies to perform her task. But if the Orcs continue to encroach on the forest, they will create a sizable stronghold that could be used to launch an invasion of Edron."

Nushala chimed in, "Before, they were simple raiding parties, divided, but there has been a culmination of the small groups into a formidable force. The recently appointed War Chief has managed to unite them under his banner and built a massive camp in the southern region of the forest." She moved towards Stellda's desk, picked up a quill, and began to scribble on some blank parchment.

She laid down the quill and presented the parchment to the party, and explained that the camp is completely surrounded by a cheval defence wall. There are four watch towers located on these walls, approximately thirty feet high, and accessed by a wooden ladder; they usually have two to three guards stationed on the platform. On the inside of the wall, approximately six guards patrol the perimeter.

There are two entrances, one on the east side and one on the south, both of which are manned by two large Orc guards. There are tents that occupy the north side of the camp, and close to the centre is a larger tent, which we believe is the War Chief's tent. The south side serves as a gathering area and features a large bonfire near the centre.

Nectarion asked Nushala, "Do you know the contingency of the camp?"

"Not all of the Orcs are there at one time, as there are several raiding parties, like the one we faced before, located all across the forest. But not including the guards and patrols, there is

33

at least an excess of twenty to thirty Orcs in the camp, more in the daytime as they prefer to raid at night."

Purvan decided to add his input, "Excuse me, but what is it that you are contemplating?"

"You still have a few days before I have completed my study of the crystal, perhaps you could assist us in dealing with the Orcs. Shala is only one person, but now, you are five." Stellda added to the discussion.

"You still expect the five of us to go up against more than forty, maybe more, Orcs?"

"Only five, yes, but not all battles need to be fought with sheer force. We will use subterfuge and cunning. Now that I have you to aid me, we can hit them from several sides and avoid the main body from escaping." Nushala said in an appealing tone.

"That is all dependent on whether we decide to commit to this endeavour," Oophaga added.

A silence filled the study as everyone allowed their minds to fill with concern and contemplation. Finally, Stellda stood up and moved towards the kettle on the stove before she broke the tension.

"True, no one is forcing you to do this, nothing wrong with being scared. But no story of a hero was ever built on staying home in safety; all the great legends told are about danger and risk, something any bard would understand." She looked tentatively at Purvan and placed her hand on his forearm, "No one ever said the calling of a hero was easy, but when we are called, we must decide whether to answer or to remain in the darkness."

Nectarion responded, "Can you give us a moment?" and he gestured to the rest of the party to form a huddle and quietly discuss the situation.

As the minutes went by, Stellda and Nushala exchanged anxious glances with each other. The party then turned back to the two and informed,

"We will answer the call, we will aid you in removing the Orc threat from the forest."

The party woke early and made their way to the kitchen for breakfast. A heavy silence filled the room as the party ate their meals. The group finished and left the table, collecting their gear. Together with Nushala, they said goodbye to Stellda and exited the tower.

Nushala explained, "It's not a long journey to the Orc camp, about a day and a half, but the forest is thick and will take time to traverse. There is a campsite that I frequent where we can spend the night before we make the final trek to the camp, arriving about midday."

The party began walking along the dirt track that led out of the grove and in a west-south-west direction. Unlike the track that led them to the tower, this track was overgrown with grass that was knee high, or in Purvan's case, chest high. The day went by smoothly and uneventfully. The party stopped for a break and a small bite to eat. The sun barely shone through the canopy, but the temperature indicated that it was now the middle of the day. Continuing through the long grass, the day ventured into the afternoon, and a slight forest chill began to cling to the party. With only a few hours of daylight left, Nushala finally led them into an opening in the forest where the foliage receded.

The area was populated with old, dilapidated stone walls that once formed buildings of what would have been a homestead. Grass grew high against the walls, ferns and forest shrubs covered the ground, and the few trees that helped fill this area allowed a bit more sunlight through than the dense canopy of before. There was a small patch of trodden grass and dirt where Nushala began to gather rocks on the ground nearby and formed a stone circle. She then began to move around the area, collecting twigs and leaves, and placing them in the centre of the circle.

"I know it's still early, but if we camp now, that trek to the camp will be better timed, and here, we are at a safe distance from being discovered."

The party milled around the site, exploring and examining the ruins for anything interesting. Nectarion sat near the newly lit fire and began working on a cloak while Pluteus studied the tomes he was gifted from Stellda: the *'Book of Tyfar'* and *'The Influence of Great Mages in Politics'* and worked on improving his Greatstaff. Oophaga wandered around aimlessly and picked some flowers that they could use in potion making. They moved towards one of the stone walls to inspect a plant when the ground beneath them suddenly gave way.

The loud noise was close enough that it startled the entire group, and they all moved towards the sound speedily.

Down in the hole, Oophaga lay on their back. Not injured as the drop was only about ten feet, but somewhat dishevelled. They looked up at the entrance, where light entered the subterranean chamber, and could see shadowy figures.

"Are you okay down there?" The sound of Pluteus' voice echoed.

"Yeah, I'm fine, just a little scuffed, but nothing I haven't dealt with before."

As they collected themself from the fall, Oophaga looked around in this small square room with stone walls. Looking up, they now noticed that they had been standing on a hatch door that must have given way under their weight. The position of the hatch, this room, and the surface ruins, this room was most likely some kind of cellar or storage room, approximately twenty feet square.

The small amount of light that entered the room from above allowed them to see that this room was practically empty, with the exception of some dried, dead grass on the floor, a few vines that had made their way down here, and, in the corner, they could see skeletal remains.

The humanoid skeleton was slumped up against the wall, its clothing old and worn but still mostly intact. By its side was a leather satchel, dusty and cracked and just near them on the other side was the skeletal remains of a small animal - a fox.

"Hang on a moment, we'll get you out," they heard from above.

"Just a moment, there is something down here."

Nectarion hovered down into the hole and lifted Oophaga and their discovery out of the ground. The party now all accounted for, returned to the campfire and seated themselves around the warm flames. Oophaga examined the satchel and found the initials "K" and "D" embossed on the flap, but it was completely empty. The skeleton had been holding a book, which seems to be a journal, also with the initials K and D bevelled into the cover with faded gold paint. They opened it and began to read it, allowing the rest of the group all listen intently.

****

Second day of Orgus, 759/FA

I rose bright and early this morning and left before the sun appeared on the horizon. This is a project that I have been planning for months, and the council has given me the 'go-ahead'. They are happy with funding half the quest, hoping I return with a well of knowledge and discoveries. I am finding it very exciting to be camping out here in the wild. I really feel like I have made great time on the first day. Although I haven't found anything, I am extremely hopeful that I will discover something in the coming days.

I can still see the mountain in the distance, off to the east. There is a slight feeling of melancholy for home, but I am on a quest and must focus on my goals.

Fourth day of Orgus, 759/FA

I have reached the outskirts of a forest today. There are no forests around the Anvil for miles, so it is interesting to see such a dense collection of trees. I am keeping the fire thoroughly stoked, as I can hear the calls of many beasts I've never heard before. It is slightly unsettling.

I must admit that I thought this might have been much easier than expected, with the first couple of days so uneventful. But I must stay vigilant.
I just heard something in the trees........

Fifth day of Orgus, 759/FA

I woke this morning to find a little friend sleeping near the fire. A fox. She has a beautiful, shiny coat and an incredible bushy tail. Wild foxes are very different from those that wander our farmlands. Those foxes always look guant and unfed.

Whatever those noises were last night, I am alive, so fortunately, it is nothing to worry about, I hope. My little fox companion has been following me all day. Perhaps I should have refrained from feeding her this morning at breakfast. Still, it is nice to have someone, even if it is a simple creature.

The forest remains difficult to traverse as it is extremely thick. I often have to backtrack as the density is impossible to break through. A few times, my companion has aided me, which I am grateful for.

Ninth day of Orgus, 759/FA

After spending the past few days in this dreadful woodland, I am pleased that I seem to be coming out the opposite side of the forest. The trees have started to thin out. Jinks is still with me (I gave her a name). My food supply is dwindling, but not seriously enough to begin to worry. I crossed a river two days ago, which helped with my water supply.

I have thought about home and returning to perhaps gather a group of adventurers and more supplies. But I also think about the recognition for completing this quest on my own. It has only been a week, but being away from people and civilisation makes it seem longer.

Thankfully, I have my compass. One of two. The other is back home. If I ever get lost, all I need to do is follow the needle. I am not much of an artist, and my map drawing is primitive. I have no real idea of distance, just how many days have passed.

Eleventh day of Orgus, 759/FA

Finally, I have cleared the forest. We are travelling through gorgeous grasslands now. It feels good to be out in the open. Jinks was dubious about continuing with me, but after surveying the land and looking at me, she decided to continue. Looking now, it seems the forest wraps around to the north of these grasslands. It would provide excellent coverage, lumber and food supplies for a newly established settlement. The Council should be excited about that.

Thirteenth day of Orgus, 759/FA

Today has been the most exciting day so far. Just as adventuring was becoming monotonous again, I have happened across a great ruin of a city. I would definitely say it was built before the First Age. There are some buildings still quite intact, and the language written on some of the walls looks ancient. I believe they used runes to write with. What delight! I do not think I will be able to sleep tonight due to the anticipation of tomorrow.

Fifteenth day of Orgus, 759/FA

Jinks and I have spent the last two days exploring the ruins. There doesn't seem to be anything that I could find overly interesting. The construction and layout do not differ so much from the current standards of home, but there is an air about it, almost like I can hear the history in these walls.

THERE ARE SEVERAL PAGES TORN OUT HERE

Fifth day of Siptimbah, 759 F/A

After travelling south for several days, we hit another forest. I suppose it is not too bad, as we have just spent the past few weeks exploring ruins and traversing grasslands. Despite these beautiful lands, I had hoped by now that I would have come across other settlements, people. Surely we can not be all that still exists in the world.

Tomorrow, we will begin to explore these new woodlands. We have been following the nearby river in order to stay replenished. Food has definitely thinned out in the past few weeks, and I have had to resort to hunting for food. The process is unsettling, but I should have realised earlier that this was a possibility. I have had to cut back on sharing with Jinks; luckily, she can hunt for her own meals. The other day, she actually bought back a hare and dumped it at my feet; she actually bought me food. She has become very special to me; she helps keep my sanity out here alone. Even though she doesn't speak, I like to imagine that she understands me to an extent.

Sixth day of Siptimbah, 759 F/A

After travelling the better part of today along the river, we came across a small lake. As we began to set up camp, I was startled by something. We had been surprised by a group of strange people. Perhaps the old gods heard my thoughts last night.

At first, both I and they were very dubious of one another. One began to speak a strange language. I noticed Jinks step forward and, to my surprise, responded. I couldn't believe my eyes.

Afterwards, the people invited me and Jinks to their camp or village. They lived in huts made of foliage and had logs circling a campfire. An individual of some importance exited a nearby hut and approached us. We were seated, and he began to speak the same language as the others had before.

I introduced myself in my own language, to which there was a pause. Then the leader responded in turn. Once we were able to converse, things became much clearer. He explained they are called druids, guardians and protectors of nature, able to use the natural energies around them to aid their cause. They refer to themselves as the Druids of Marr and that this forest is their domain to protect, the Forest of Marr.

One of their abilities was to be able to talk to animals, which is why they didn't kill me on site. My little fox friend vouched for me and said I was of good character.

Twelfth day of Siptimbah 759 F/A

I have spent the better part of the week here with these druids. They are extremely fascinating people. I have been learning about their culture and customs. They even showed me a few survival techniques for travelling the wilds. I explained to them my quest and my own people, where I am from and how we live. They found it difficult to comprehend, not because they are dimwitted but because they never take more than they need to survive. They are one with the land; they don't live on it, they are part of it.

After talking about the different types of magic that both our people use, they explained that their magic comes from someone called the Nuturing Maiden, a god of old.
They showed me their sacred tree, a large, bulky redwood tree, which apparently talks to them. Suppose you believe in such things. I played along, not wishing to offend.
They were also kind enough to impart to me the gift of animal speech. I am so excited to finally be able to converse with Jinks and find out what she has been thinking.

Fifteenth day of Siptimbah, 759 F/A

Jinks and I have been travelling through the Forest of Marr
for the past few days. I am not as ecstatic as I was a few days
ago. While I can converse with Jinks now, her intelligence does
not allow her to understand the complexities of people.
Nonetheless, it is still refreshing to be able to talk to someone
while on my own. She is still my dear friend.

We have made camp near another small lake, smaller than the
one near the druid village. It is quiet here. I can not hear the
sounds of the forests I have camped in before. Jinks doesn't
seem unsettled by it so much. She explains that this forest is
just as much foreign to her as it is to me.

Seventeenth day of Siptimbah, 759 F/A

After a month of travelling, it has finally happened: we are in
danger. We are being pursued by several green-skinned
man-beasts. I have not seen the likes before, but I believe they
are Trolls or Orcs, from descriptions in books I have read.

Jinks and I have remained hidden for nearly two days now. We
found a small area of ruins, a secret chamber with a hatch. I

used what the druids taught me to cover our tracks and mask the hatch. We have enough food for a few days, if we can just wait it out until they go away. Surely they will grow tired and leave.

Twentieth day of Siptimbah, 759 F/A

I can still hear the beasts above us. I can't understand their language. Mostly grunts and growls.

My stomach growls. I have rationed out the supplies for the two of us. We have a day or two before we finish them off. Hopefully, we will have made a break for it by then.

Twenty-second day of Siptimbah, 759 F/A

They are relentless; they have not stopped. The food is gone, and it is cold. It must be now, or we will perish here.
I am scared.

Twenty-fifth day of Siptimbah, 759 F/A

I am in sorrow. The food was gone. I burnt the maps and some of the pages of my journal, I know not which. At this point, I don't believe it matters.

The food was gone. I can hear them above. I am scared.

Jinks......

Twenty-sev......

******

Oophaga closed the book and looked over at the remains of the individual and the fox. The group sat around the campfire in silence, absorbing the tale they had just heard.

"I think it would be prudent to have a watch active tonight, just in case," Nushala suggested to the party.

"We should give them a proper burial," Oophaga added as they stood and moved to a spot away from the fire.

"I will assist you." Nectarion expressed.

By now, the sun had set, and the stars littered the night sky in abundance. It was only a few hours since the evening, but the party were slightly melancholy and decided to bed down for the night. Purvan was quietly talking with Nushala as the others lay their heads down, hoping to get an early start in the morning.

Chapter Three

The party woke just as the first rays of the sun broke over the horizon. They remained quiet and ate a small cold breakfast rather than rekindling the fire. They packed their belongings together and headed out again. Nushala moved through the tree tops, scouting ahead sixty feet. Her companion, a black hawk named Jessa, flew by her side.

Along the way, the party noticed signs of disturbances in the forest, felled trees and the carcasses of animals. Nushala became quite disturbed by this.

"This is devastating, unwarranted. These animals didn't have to die."

The party collected itself after witnessing the destruction and remained silent for hours until they finally reached the forest on the outskirts of the Orc camp. By now, it was the middle of the day, and the temperature had peaked despite the shade of the cool forest. Nushala sent Jessa to survey the camp and its current status. When she returned, the black hawk communicated to Nushala what she had scouted.

"At the east entrance, in the gathering area, a large fire roars with three spit roasts straddling it. The South entrance is obstructed by a group of a dozen Orcs training. The towers contain two guards each, two Orcs at each entrance, and there are six Orcs on patrol around the perimeter. There also seems to be a small contingent guarding one of the tents on the western side of the camp."

"It sounds too busy to attempt anything at the moment; we should wait until nightfall when they send out their patrols." Purvan assumed.

"How will you approach the situation?" Nushala asked.

The Plan (looking at the map): we should take out the guards in the two eastern towers, exposing this side. The guards at the eastern entrance should be easy to deal with after that. Pluteus and I will create a mist cloud around the towers to blind them. Next, Nectarion, you fly Oophaga to that tower and relieve the Orcs of their watch, while Pluteus and I will repeat the same on the other tower. At this point, Nushala, you fire some flame arrows at those tents and set them alight, specifically the main tent here (pointing at the large tent in the centre of the camp).

Once there is confusion and disarray, we can make our way to the west side and repeat the process on the other towers. Once the tents are ablaze, we can begin to set the barricades around the camp on fire, trapping the entire force in a blazing prison.

"We should move out of range of the camp and the towers, to avoid detection. There is a location just south of the camp, about a hundred and fifty feet away, where we can wait until nightfall. I can send Jessa out periodically to keep us updated on the camp's status."

Purvan concluded, "Fantastic, now all we need is some dice."

The group found a large shrubbery where they crawled underneath for camouflage. They huddled up and did their best to remain quiet for the rest of the day, in anticipation of the hour of attack.

Jessa flew in and out of the forest every few hours, returning to inform her companion of the camp's movements, raiding parties' returning and departing. The numbers fluctuated, but not as much as hoped. When the sun set and the night sky took hold, Jessa came back with another report, indicating no substantial change in the number occupying the camp.

"We need to make sure that their forces a spread thin, otherwise it will be too many for us to contend with." Nectarion voiced concern.

"We need to attack; the Orcs have become too bolstered. If they continue to increase in numbers, nothing we do will make any difference," pleaded Nushala.

"It's still early, let us wait a few more hours, when the camp should be unsuspecting," Pluteus suggested.

The hours ticked by, and the night's cold began to drop substantially. The group huddled closer to keep warm, as there was no fire to warm themselves by. Jessa flew in again with another update. Everyone but Oophaga on watch is asleep. Jessa went up to her and tried to communicate. She jumped on the spot, on her two skinny bird legs and moved towards Nushala, implying that Oophaga come over.

Oophaga woke Nushala, and Jessa communicated with her friend. They woke the others, and Nushala relayed to the party Jessa's report.

"Apparently, there is a small company of people in shiny skin making their way towards the west wall."

51

At that moment, there was a loud uproar coming from the direction of the camp. The party jumped to their feet and ran out of the shrubbery towards the Orc camp. Arriving at the tree line, the party looked at the camp and noticed a small company of what appeared to be soldiers, knights, in full plate armour, had made an opening in the barricade and entered the camp. They were heavily engaged in combat with the Orcs, who had now exited their tents and were returning blows with the company of knights.

"What do we do?"

"Who are they?"

"Should we assist?"

Questions were flying out from everyone.

"We wanted a distraction; we have been gifted." Nushala moved towards camp, looking back at the others, "Come on, this is our chance."

The others looked at each other with resolve, determination and a smile on their faces. They prepared themselves and shot off to their positions.

Orcs, knights, swords clashed, shields pushed back against metal, and the battle in the gathering area was now in full motion. In the background, the Orc guards on the towers fired arrows at the battle. Just as they loosed a few arrows, a mist began to gather around their proximity. In moments, the top of the tower was completely covered in fog. Across the way, the other tower experienced the same effect. The Orc guards on the tower platform began grunting, confused and blinded, and aimlessly continued to fire arrows in the general direction of the battle.

From the tree line, a small bright light flew through the air as Nushala fired lit arrows towards the camp's tents. One, two, three. Each one hit one of the smaller tents. Nushala was determined to hit her mark, lit another arrow, and arched her bow, hoping it was at the right angle.

WOOSH.

In what felt like an eternity, the arrow coasted through the air, and a slight breeze passed by Nushala, making her anxious. The arrow finished its course and disappeared behind one of the tents near the main one.

Nectarion picked up Oophaga and flew over to one of the towers and dropped them down on the platform amid the mist cloud. Using their senses, they determined where the two Orc guards were and summoned vines to entangle them. The vines wrapped around them and tightened. Ooph could hear them grunting, almost squealing, until the vines had fully tightened, then silence.

Meanwhile, at the other watch tower, the two Orc guards had stood down from firing and tried to push the fog away, at which point, a Halfling bard had made his way up the ladder, followed closely by his mushroom friend. They reached the top and climbed up on the platform, and both cast their spells and engulfed the Orcs in fire. Pluteus used his Greatstaff to focus his attack, and one Orc that was set alight, flew off the platform and fell onto the barricade below, ending with a large log penetrating its abdomen.

At the tree line, Nushala stood disappointed at her last shot, only to find, after a moment, that she saw flames climb higher as the main tent began to burn. She then looked to her right and noticed a stray flying fireball hit the wall, the fire spreading to the wooden structure, lighting it up. She collected herself and made her way down to the eastern entrance. She peered inside the gate to locate the guards, but there were none. She moved gingerly into the camp, looking at the tops of the watch towers covered in mist. She could see a large, bee-like individual carrying a small pinky-blue-skinned frog, carrying a sword across the way to the main battle. At that moment, coming up to her side were Purvan and Pluteus. A nod of acknowledgement is given to proceed.

Gathered together again, the five companions stood on the edge of the battle, looking on intently, waiting for an opening to join the fray. First, Nectarion and Pluteus entered, with Nectarion swinging his Hallowed axe and Pluteus engulfing the enemy in flame. Oophaga's form slightly convulsed as they became a wolf and ran towards the onslaught. Purvan looked at Nushala, and she looked back at him. They ran in, arrows flew, and the sound of music filled the air.

One particular knight who looked like a commander or an officer was making his way through the enemy forces, swinging his longsword and taking off heads, running Orcs through. Close behind him, another individual with lavender coloured skin moved in unison with him, a magnificent ballet of blades and blood. The main force now neutralised, the company of knights met face to face with the party. A split-second pause in which both looked at each other, and then they all returned to fighting the Orcs.

The two groups stood together now amongst a pile of slain Orcs, and looked towards five large, brutish-looking Orcs, moving towards them, overbearing. There is another look between the knights and the party, and with another burst of conviction and adrenaline, the two groups moved forward and attacked them. Coming up behind the brutes is the largest Orc that could exist, adorned in bone jewellery, beads, and animal parts. Atop his ugly head was the skull of a deer with its antlers, covered in paint and ornaments. He joined the line of his warriors and rushed into the carnage. The two allied forces, almost overpowered by brute Orcish strength, paused for a moment, and a glare between them initiated the final push. The two commanding knights subdued two of the Orc brutes. Purvan, Oophaga and Pluteus subdued the other three, ending their existence, and in the middle, the large bee-like entity of Nectarion pivoted in a hundred and eighty degrees, swinging his axe and driving it through the War Chief's torso, cutting him in half. It slid slowly to one side, and the body fell to the ground in two.

The two groups stood there, tired and somewhat battered but overly okay. The entire camp was now in flames as the tents and half the barricades that made up the defence around the camp were burning. The silhouette of over a dozen people in front of the flaming blaze, against the forest and starry night sky.

Chapter Four

The party and the company of soldiers stood side by side, staring at the burning Orc camp against the night sky. A moment of respite passed, and the commanding soldier approached the party.

"I want to thank you for aiding us in the battle. I don't know who you are, but I am happy to call you a friend for now."

A male Elf, about six feet tall with lightly tanned white skin, chiselled face and muscular arms with long, blonde, silvery hair done up in a ponytail, stands before the party. He was wearing shiny but dented, half-plate attire with red leather under-armour and black trousers and boots. He also wore a red cloak draped over his shoulder with some sort of black insignia, obscured by grime. In his hand, he carried a longsword, the hilt embellished with jewel inlay. The light of the flames hit the gems and lit up his face, enhancing his charm.

"You are welcome, but I feel it is *we* who should be thanking you," added Purvan.

"Intriguing. My manners, let me introduce myself and my company. I am Sir Renart of Pinecrest. This is my lieutenant, Teffenie of Nirian and my men, the Knights of Pinecrest."

The female Infernis, second in command, standing five and a half feet tall, with lavender skin, shoulder-length hair, two medium, curved dark blue horns that protrude from the front of her dark purple hairline and deep silver eyes with no pupils. Wearing custom-made half-plate to account for her ample bosom, her black leather body suit was made to reveal her buttocks, and she sported two gauntlets on her otherwise exposed, slim lavender arms. Knee-high leather boots with shin-plates covered her lower legs before her smooth lavender skin was exposed again. She, too, has a cloak draped over her shoulder, but it is a dull forest green, and she carries two shortswords with curved blades. The hilts were made of standard materials, but of a fine quality.

The rest of the company looked similar to Renart but of a more standard appearance, depicting their station. Their armour and weapons were of decent quality, and they did not wear cloaks. They wore helms, some with face guards. They seemed to be made up of mostly Elves and Humans, and one other Infernis.

"Well, my name is Purvan, these are my companions, Pluteus, Nectarion, Oophaga and Nushala."

"A pleasure, good sir. My company and I are going to remain here for the rest of the night before we head out in the morning. If you and your party are not heading out, perhaps it would be prudent to camp near each other or even together." Sir Renart gestured back towards where he and his company originated.

The parties agreed, and the two groups made their way through the forest just a small distance from the burning Orc camp. Nushala remained behind for a while to ensure the fire didn't spread to the forest.

Renart's men set up a fire and laid their bedrolls out, and the party did the same just off to the side of the company. They did not prepare any food as it was quite late in the night, but wine skins got passed around for the company to drink from. Renart's men took up seating around the fire and continued to drink as they recalled their battle in glorious revere. Sir Renart and Teffenie joined them, and eventually the party sat down amongst them.

Once settled, Renart turned to the party and asked,

"So what was the reason for your group being here? Were you sent to engage the Orcs?"

"Our Elvish companion, who is a resident and guardian of this forest, asked us for aid, and we agreed," Nectarion explained.

"The Orcs had become very troublesome, and we wanted to do what we could to help," Pluteus added.

"What about yourselves? What reason did you have to infiltrate the Orc camp?" Purvan queried.

Renart looked at the party with a slight look of grief.

"The Orcs had raided our village and kidnapped some of our people. Our mission was one of rescue only, and we had not intended to engage the enemy. While the Orcs are no longer a major threat, thanks to your assistance, we only managed to rescue some of the hostages."

Renart pointed over to where three women and five children were huddled together, beaten, bruised and in shock.

"Our condolences, Sir Renart. It seems we were in the right place at the right time," stated Purvan.

"Look at us being saddened," Renart announced, "we should be rejoicing. The mission was a success, still, and we achieved an additional goal. Along with new friends." He took a swig from his wine skin, and the company all cheered and returned the favour. Teffenie turned to Renart and said something in a sincere tone using an unknown language. Renart looked back at the party and asked,

"So, my friends, where do you hail from?"

"We come from Edron, just the other side of the Redwood forest." Purvan pointed to the east, the direction they ventured from.

"Edron, you say, I don't believe we have ever heard of that land." Renart confoundedly stated. "Is it ruled by a king?"

"No, we have Lord Governors who rule the land, three of them to be exact," explained Nectarion.

"It sounds fascinating. Perhaps now that the Orcs have been cleared out of the forest, we can begin to explore these lands in the east and make new allies. The Orcs have made it difficult to traverse these woods for quite a while."

"What about where you are from?" rousingly inquired Pluteus.

"We come from the kingdom of Tarin Marr," and Renart pointed west. "Specifically, my company and I come from the village of Pinecrest, just a few kilometres outside Orcwood, which is what we call this forest."

The group looked at each other with excitement.

"It is amusing that we have not heard of your kingdom either," said Nectarion.

"Then this is even more cause for celebration, the first contact between two peoples," Renart replied. "I do not know where your journey will take you, but if you are ever in the kingdom of Tarin Marr, you are more than welcome, especially in Pinecrest."

The two groups cheered again and took another swig from their wine skins.

During this interaction, Teffenie had remained quite stoic but listened intently. At the same time, Oophaga had been entranced by the Inferni's beauty, never seeing anything like her before. When the main conversation had subsided and most of the soldiers had retired for the night to their bedrolls, Oophaga approached Teffenie, and from out of their palm, a beautiful flower magically appeared, a red and blue orchid of some kind, native to Oophaga's grove from whence they came.

"I have seen great beauty in this land, my lavender friend, but you are now the most beautiful I have ever laid eyes upon."

Oophaga handed Teffenie the flower, and she received it awkwardly. An individual of military background, of soldiers and combat, she was not accustomed to such a tender gesture. It was obvious to Ooph that Teffenie was not used to the gentleness that they were presenting. Teffenie blushed with embarrassment as Ooph tucked the flower behind her ear and traced along her jaw with a gentle touch. Ooph stared deeply into Teffenies's deep, silvery eyes, their reflection appearing in them.

"Your eyes twinkle like the stars. They put the moon to shame". Oophaga softly mentioned to her.

Renart looked across at Oophaga with a humorous smile. "You'll have to excuse the lieutenant; she has been a soldier for most of her life and is not used to being showered with affection as such."

Oophaga gently smiled at Teffenie and returned to their companions. As they do, they hear laughter from the soldiers and Sir Renart.

Ooph yelled over their shoulder, "You're just jealous no one likes you."

The laughing paused for a moment and then reignited, even louder.

As the camp settled into slumber, Pluteus studied the tomes he received from Stellda, and Nushala had finally joined them. She rolled out her bedding next to Purvan's and began to take a rest when Purvan turned to look at her.

"I hope I didn't make you feel uncomfortable last night at the ruins?"

"You did not, I was just caught off guard a little." She paused a moment and continued. "I have lived most of my life in these woods with the company of the trees and the animals. Besides Stellda, I have never interacted with anyone."

"You've never been with someone, intimately?" he asked

"No," she sharply responded.

Purvan moved in closer to Nushala. She was hesitant, not knowing what was happening and then he began to whisper in her ear,

"Oh, Ranger, you're in danger
But never fear, for I am near
In the forest brush, we need not rush
Patience is a virtue, as feelings grew
The rush of battle, the death rattle
To save the forest, no need for modest
Come sit by my side, and let your emotions slide
The night is long, Whispered song
We have tonight, it feels so right
Share with me, let us be we."

Nushala slowly turned to face Purvan and stared at him for a moment with a blank expression on her face. And just as if magic had worked its words into her heart, she pounced on Purvan.

The morning arrived, and both groups were slow to rise after the late-night battle. They gathered some breakfast, and the smell of food cooking filled the camp. The night watches found no contest, any renegade Orcs long gone. Nushala and Purvan were spooning in his bedroll, and Pluteus, with a book resting on his fungal face, snored lightly. Oophaga was near the fire and glanced over at Teffenie. She returned an awkward grin.

With the meal consumed, the camp is packed up, and both groups are prepared to depart on their separate ways.

"I guess this is goodbye for now," Renart stated as he extended his hand out in friendship. "Don't be a stranger, come visit."

The party all extended their hands in recognition and bid the Pinecrest company farewell. Oophaga gave Teffenie a small kiss on the back of her hand before joining their companions and heading back to the tower and Stellda.

The trek back through the forest was full of life, as if the forest itself had been renewed and knew that the corruption of the Orcs was gone. A few times, the party swore they could have seen an Orc but believed it to be a trick of the light. They camped again at the ruins, Nushala and Purvan bedding together as the others went about some chores before bedding down as well.

The morning woke, and the party was better rested after this night compared to the last. The dirt path began to show again as the overgrowth subsided. The temperature peaked as it reached the midday hour and began to drop again just as the party entered the grove in the afternoon. The sight of Stellda's tower before them was a relief, as they were all yearning for a proper meal and a comfortable sleep.

The party walked through the familiar door and made their way up the spiral staircase. Nushala announced their arrival.

"Stellda dear, are you there?" There was quiet.

The party hastened their speed and came to the study and saw Stellda, sitting in her armchair by the window, motionless. Nushala and the rest of the group rushed to her side and startled her.

"Stellda, are you okay?" Stellda woke, groggy from sleep but looking exhausted.

"What's happened? Is something wrong?" the party asked.

In broken speech, Stellda attempted to explain,

"A vision......I have seen something..........darkness." She stood and began to move about the room, worried, stricken.

"I am afraid I have to deliver the crystal myself. I must go to Westhold and speak with the Novum Arcanum; I need counsel."

She began to gather some belongings and a travel pack, shoving the items into the pack in a distressed manner.

Pluteus interjected, "But I thought you wished for us to deliver the crystal?"

"That was before; things have drastically changed. Your services are no longer required; you have confirmation of delivery, return to your Lord, well done."

The party huddled together and quietly discussed the situation and then decided.

"We may not be a service in regards to the crystal, but it may still be beneficial if we at least travel together, until you reach Westhold, safely. A thief has already attempted to steal the crystal back in Goshan."

Stellda halted and looked at the party with surprise.

"You didn't tell me that before. This could be more serious than I thought? Alright, you can travel with me to Westhold."

The party calmed Stellda somewhat and convinced her to wait till morning before venturing out. Purvan kept an eye on her with Nushala. She was restless and spent most of the night tossing and turning in her bed, muttering various phrases such as *eternal darkness, they are coming, the end of life.*

Before the light of the sun touched the tower, the group rose and gathered itself, ready. Stellda stood at the window near her armchair, staring out into nothingness, deep in thought.

"I will not be going with you". Nushala explained. "I must remain and tend to the forest; the animals will be returning now that the Orcs have been defeated, and I must be there to assist them."

She kneeled to her Halfling friend,

"I will miss you, my love. Please don't be gone long. My place is here, but if my yearning for you begins to take hold of me, I will come find you, and we can return to live here until the end of our days." She gave Purvan a small kiss on his cheek.

Stellda looked on at this scene, somewhat surprised at first; a flash of hurt crossed her face, but she shook it off; her mind wandering back to the situation at hand as the dark dreams continued to persist. The party turned away and headed towards the forest road that would take them back into Edron and the Silverleaf road to Westhold.

Chapter Five

A few days passed as the party made their way back to Edron. The nights were peaceful for all but Stellda, who was continuously restless during the night. On the second night, Purvan attempted to help her rest by singing to her. His calm, soft tone magically eased her troubled mind.

"Are you okay, my friend?" he asked.

She nodded slightly, indicating her ease.

"Do you wish to talk about it?"

She looked up at Purvan with the gravest of faces.

"It is coming, but I don't know exactly what; it is simply darkness."

"Is it a prophecy?"

"Stuffed if I know, I poured through my whole library and found countless prophecies and premonitions about a coming darkness, which is why I am somewhat stressed, who knows which one it is."

"What did you see?" Purvan asked gingerly.

"I saw a darkness, followed by demons, or maybe they were devils or both, hellish armies marching across the lands, enslaving people, harvesting their souls for power. It is the usual forte of those foul creatures, always wanting the souls of mortals to increase their power."

Purvan's face now slightly resembled Stellda's as a realisation washed over him.

"This is why I must go and speak to the mages in Westhold. The Novum Arcanum are the most elite magic users in the land, and perhaps we can determine more details between the two of us."

Stellda finally rolled back over and rested her head down. "Thank you for helping ease my thoughts. I will need a good rest for when we reach the city."

Purvan placed his hand on her shoulder in reassurance and smiled. He then returned to his bedroll and drifted off to sleep.

After three days of travelling through the Redwood forest, the party reached the signpost that they had originally come across over a week ago. The sign pointing north, Westhold 25km, the party began the last leg of the journey to Westhold.

Westhold is very much like Goshan, not as big, but still quite large, as it is one of the three biggest cities in Edron.

While Goshan sports the two-tone blues, Westhold's banner colours are red with puce.

Like the other cities, the Great Keep is in the centre as well as the Hall of Mages, where the Novum Arcanum reside, surrounded by a wall with towers. Outside the wall are the market and commerce districts, where you will find food, supplies, specialty shops, restaurants and boutiques and on the outskirts are the residential districts where the denizens of Westhold live.

As the party entered the city, they saw the citizens in revelry, as it was the Autumn celebrations. A three-day festival that happened at the end of the first month of the season. The city was decorated with banners and streamers of browns, oranges, reds and yellows. The shops were selling all manner of items and clothing for the season, food vendors were selling mooncakes, pumpkin-based meals, chicken, turkey and duck skewers, taro and lotus roots, warm nuts and crab meat from the coast. Minstrels were playing seasonal music, and the people were dancing in the street. Stellda turned to the party.

"Well, thank you for the company and escort, but I no longer require your assistance. I will head to the Hall of Mages and consult with them. I will come to find you to tell you the result. Go, enjoy the festival, you have earned it."

The party looked on as Stellda continued towards the walled part of the city and looked at each other momentarily, then began to wander off in search of respite.

As the party strolled through the festivities, they began to sample the various cuisines available. Nectarion decided to fill his hands with meat skewers of chicken, turkey and duck, glazed in honey and lemon. He had never tried this type of food before and immediately fell in love with it. He bought more and caught up with the rest of his friends, all four hands full of skewered meat.

The party spied a tavern across the way, the front wide open with the doors pulled right across to one side. Above the entrance was a sign saying 'The Fancy Rabbit' and a small image of a rabbit wearing a top hat. The party entered the tavern, and the walls were covered in art depicting rabbits in formal wear and various mounts of rabbits wearing top hats, monocles and doll-sized fancy attire. There were almost a hundred people in the tavern, the party made their way through the crowd and found themselves a place to sit at the back of the establishment, the patrons in full festivities, enjoying drink, food and music from a small band of minstrels on a tiny raised stage across the room from the party.

As the hours passed, midday became the afternoon, and the sun could be seen setting behind the buildings in the west. The barkeep lit the lamps around the tavern, and the fragrance of the evening meal could be smelled coming from the kitchen.

Just when the party had reached a state of full relaxation, enjoying the celebrations, a loud voice was heard at the front of the establishment. The entire tavern, music and all, went quiet as six small Ribbets crossed the threshold of the entrance and the lead Ribbet leapt up onto a vacant stool near the bar. The silence was broken when he spoke.

"We are currently looking for a female Ribbet who is responsible for murder. Our investigations have led us to this establishment. Are there any Ribbets in here? Could you please present yourself for identification?"

The patrons stared at him and each other, confounded at his request. In the corner, a Galapa that had been sitting peacefully and enjoying a meal, stood and walked over to the Ribbets.

The party in the back, behind the large crowd, looked at Oophaga with concern and on their face was worry and panic. Without any more hesitation, Pluteus and Nectarion stealthily took Ooph at the back door of the tavern.

"We'll meet you back at the entrance to the inner city." Nectarion quietly relayed to Purvan.

The Galapa saw the female Ribbet, that is Oophaga, come in earlier with their companions and had been watching them since. They were not causing any trouble, but the Galapa did find it odd that an Apis-fae, a Halfling, a Ribbet and something that resembled a giant mushroom were together.

69

The female Galapa who approached the Ribbets stands just over five feet tall, with brown skin and flecks of green throughout. Her shell was trimmed with gold and the colour of jade across the main shell; opalescent, the colour shifted in the light. She wore a loose, flowy, swashbuckler-style shirt with roughly sewn sections from being cut or snagged, a leather jerkin with rusty buckles for aesthetics, and a short split skirt to show her femininity. Upon her head, she wore a faded blue Kangol hat that almost looked grey.

The barkeep piped up,

"Alright mate, stop breakin' up the party, will ya, nick off."

Finally, the Galapa reached the Ribbet, standing over him still despite being on a stool, threw her hat off and said,

"There is no one here fitting that description, so your business here is finished."

The Ribbet took a slight gulp and croaked nervously. He jumped down and moved the stool to the wall near the bar, where he removed some parchment from his pack and fastened it to the wood. It was a Wanted Poster of a female Ribbet resembling Oophaga. With '**WANTED**' written in big black capital letters at the top and the bottom, Oophaga Pumilio - reward given. The Ribbet then jumped down from the stool and announced,

"If you see this individual, please report it to the local authorities," and with that, he and his party exited the tavern, and the patrons returned to their drinks, and the band struck up the music again.

Purvan, who had remained in the tavern to witness the proceedings, went across to the poster and removed it. The barkeep slipped him a look of caution and concern but said nothing. The

Galapa remained vigilant at the entrance of the tavern, ensuring that the Ribbets were not loitering around.

About half an hour later, Purvan stood up from his seat, finished his drink and left the Fancy Rabbit. He began to walk down the now quiet street of the city. Most of the stalls had closed down for the night, and the city denizens retired to their homes. A few drunken stragglers slowly hobbled along, most likely making their way home or perhaps to a quiet place to sleep it off. For a moment, Purvan stopped and had a feeling that someone might be following him. He paused and looked around, but saw nobody and then continued on his way.

He finally reached the entrance at the wall that allowed access to the inner city, the Keep and the Hall of Mages.

"Hey, where are you?" Purvan whispered loudly to his friends.

"Over here."

In the shadows, just inside the entrance, Purvan's companions came into the light of the moon. Purvan pushed them back into the shadows, cautiously looking about to ensure no one was watching.

"Okay, what the hell was all that about?" he asked, removing the wanted poster from his person and presenting it to the party.

They looked at it, barely able to make it out in the shadow, but saw that it resembled Oophaga. They all stared at their froggish friend.

In their eyes, a noticeable look of dread had taken over them. This was something from their past that they had not yet revealed to their new comrades, as they didn't know whether they could trust them. They took a breath and spoke quietly.

"It is me they are looking for," they admitted.

"Are you a murderer?" a shocked Pluteus inquired.

"No, I swear, I did not commit any murder; this is a lie."

"Do you know these people?" Purvan asked them.

"Yes, I do, they come from my village, the grove I called home."

Nectarion looked at Oophaga with a pause. He could sense something wasn't right and asked them.

"Ooph, I can tell you are being honest, but I don't believe you are telling us the entire truth. I understand that. But if you want us to help you, you are going to have to trust us, if not now, soon."

They looked up at their bee-like friend with reservation. At that moment, the party heard a noise, feet shuffling from around the corner. A large, shadowy figure is seen closing the distance between it and the party. Nectarion pulled his Hallowed axe out at the ready and thrust it slightly forward, making contact with its mark. The shadowy form moved forward a few steps into the light, and standing there is the female Galapa from the tavern, the point of Necatarion's axe sitting on her plastron.

"Oops, you got me," she remarked sarcastically.

"I know you, you are the turtle person from the tavern." Purvan stated, "What are you doing here?"

"Well, I wasn't satisfied with just telling those frogs to leave. I felt the need to follow up on the issue and make sure you were okay."

"Why are you so interested in the 'issue'?" he continued to question.

"Even though you seem an odd bunch, I could tell that you are not criminals. Whatever the circumstances, I'm sure there must be a reasonable explanation." The Galapa turned and looked at Oophaga.

Purvan approached the large, turtle person and circled her, sizing her up. He looked at his companions and at Ooph and finally said,'

"Okay, we accept your assistance, whatever you can provide. My name is Purvan, these are my friends Pluteus, Nectarion and of course Oophaga."

"My name is Minorha Whispersea, but most just call me Minny. Now, first thing, let us remove ourselves from the public eye. My home is a little way, but it is secluded, and we will be safe there, and we can rest."

Their newly employed guide, Minorha, led them through the back streets of Westhold to a small alleyway where they found the front door to her abode. She unlocked the door and entered the small home; the party followed.

The main front room had a small table and two tree stumps for seating. At the back, where a kitchen area would most likely be, was a large rock pool with fresh water, algae and kelp lining the side. A small alcove was off to the left, where a hammock was hanging from the reinforced timber beams of the ceiling. The walls of the abode are decorated with a few ornaments such as a ship wheel, a whaling spear and other various maritime implements.

73

It was dark in here, and Minorha lit a couple of lamps that were sitting on the table. She left one and hung the other in the corner of the room at the back, near the pool, from a hook in the wall.

It was late in the night. Ooph was still shaken by the experience. Pluteus decided to take them into the alcove with the hammock and keep them company while they tried to get some sleep. Purvan and Necatrion decided to sit down with Minny and have a conversation. However, it was Necatrion that did most of the talking.

He explained how he held an important position of justice and balance in his kingdom of Aurisolis and was an aide and close confidant to Queen Aurianna of his people. She met her demise in a terrible attack on the hive by Vespi-Fae assassins. Now her daughter, Mellivara, rules their people and has tasked Nectarion with finding her mother's assassins.

Purvan talked about his life as well in short form. Grew up in a life of luxury before attending the *Shaw School of Philosophy*. Afterwards, he travelled a bit until his talents landed him an exalted position as Lord Obo's personal bard. He resided in Goshan, where he had a penthouse just inside the Great Keep's walls.

Minorha, on the other hand, was somewhat reluctant to be as forthcoming. She mentioned that she has spent most of her life on the sea, working with or for the Terrapin Syndicate. Then about ten years ago, she left her life and found her way here to Westhold, where she worked as a crowd moderator at the Fancy Rabbit.

Eventually, the party took to their beds and let sleep take them once again, with a sense of security and safety in their new friend's home.

The party woke the next morning, a little after the sun had risen. After partaking in a small breakfast, as Oophaga was still recovering from the night before and was not overly fussed on eating, and the others were anxious to set out and find some answers as to the whereabouts of Ooph's brethren.

Ooph had still not given any more information as to the situation, still yet to fully trust their fellow adventurers. So after deciding to leave Pluteus with Ooph at Minny's home, Purvan, Nectarion, and Minorha headed out to investigate.

Minny suggested that they talk to a contact she has in the Underground, an informant. She led the others through town, the citizens already en masse for the final day of the Autumn Festival, and eventually reached a small building that looked boarded up. Minny led them around the back to a passageway that led down. Purvan recognised the familiar marking of the Underground, practically hidden and in the script of the Thieves' Cant.

"I see you are familiar with the Underground. Do you work for them?"

Turning to the Halfling, Minny replied, "Of course not, but the Fancy Rabbit is a regular place for said members to visit."

"So the Fancy Rabbit is like neutral ground for criminals, a place to wheel and deal."

"What do you take me for?" Minny inserted, "I am no criminal, the tavern is just a tavern, and it has a good reputation for fine ales and excellent meals. Those who belong to the

Underground are more than welcome, but they know that while I'm there, they should not try anything. Some have, and that is how I became familiar with certain members."

The group fell silent as they continued to walk along the long tunnel that was the passage to the Underground.

After about fifteen minutes of moving through this dimly lit tunnel, passing a few homeless people, beggars, and a couple of shady characters who were just lolling around, giving the party a look that made them feel uneasy, a light could be seen in the distance. As the three moved closer, it got brighter, and commotion could be heard.

The party made its way further down, and they began to hear noise, and a pungent smell hit their noses, which reminded them of BBQ. Finally, after making their way to the end of the corridor, they saw a light. They passed through an archway, and the noise that was heard was now a mass of people from all walks of life before them. This was the Underground Market.

There was a small area before the three companions where they stood, about twenty feet square, and there were four pathways that shot off in different directions, intersecting the stalls and wooden stands that made up the market. There was a hustle and bustle as everyone was moving about, making deals and peddling their stolen goods. Purvan and Nectarion looked in awe and saw a few food vendors cooking meat skewers, which produced the smell they had picked up just before. Nectarion went over to buy some when Minny pulled him back.

"Don't wander down here. If you make a wrong move, you are dealt with swiftly, see." Minny gestured behind them, and standing there were two muscular Drakona, one a dusty black colour and the other a metal-looking one, like the colour of iron. They don't move, but they were armed and armoured. The party now noticed that in this nearby vicinity, all eyes were now on them. They were definitely out of place here. The way they presented themselves, the attire they wore, they did not belong, and everyone was wary of the three standing at the entrance to the Underground.

Minny moved first, and the others followed in close behind, cautiously making their way through the market area. After a few moments, Minny came to a halt, and Purvan and Nectarion bumped into the back of her. They turned to look at where they had stopped, and Minny was there, facing the stall next to them. Standing behind the table of what appeared to be various items of extrinsic value was a weasely little man dressed in attire that might have been found on a boag, an individual with little wealth but who dresses and acts as if they were part of high society. Their clothing looked formal but was of low quality and somewhat tacky. He looked up at the massive green entity that is Minorha, towering over him.

"Hello Jerry, how's business?"

Snivelly and nervous, with a slight tittle, he replied, "Ah, my pleasure, Minny, business is good." he finished with a gulp.

"I'll make this quick and 'worth your while'. I am looking for information on a group of six Ribbet-folk. They are searching for an individual accused of murder. Do you know anything?"

He moved a little closer, straightened up a bit more and acquired some confidence in his demeanour, rubbing the thumb, fore and middle fingers of his hand together, symbolising payment for services. Minorha reached for her coin pouch and pulled out two gold coins, handing them to the Human man.

"*Yesss*, there is talk of frog people that come to town, looking for one of their own, a murderer, yes, that is what I heard. Did they come to the Rabbit, did they?"

"They did. Can you tell me where they come from or maybe where I can find them?"

"Definitely not from Westhold, somewhere far in the north, I believe."

"Do they have a place here in the city, where they stay?"

Jerry rubbed his fingers together once more, and reluctantly, Minny handed him another gold coin.

"No, they don't have a place in the city; they leave and come back." And with that, Jerry turned back to his stall and finished, "Pleasure doing business with you as usual, Minny. Hope to see you never again," he said with a smirky grimace.

The three looked at each other, and Minny turned to walk out.

"Come on, you two, I need a drink."

Sitting back at the Fancy Rabbit, Minny, Purvan, and Nectarion sat enjoying a brew, four elderly citizens sat by themselves at other various tables, and the tavern was quite depressing early in the morning. The barkeep came over,

"What's got your daddle all twisted up?"

"Very funny, Bazz." Minny snapped back, "We have been busy all morning trying to work out *umph*."

Purvan, sitting next to her, elbowed her in the side, which hurt him and only nudged her, but the desired result was achieved.

Barry, usually called Bazz, a simple barkeep, was not an idiot.

"Is this to do with what happened yesterday?"

The three looked up at him.

"Of course it does, what else would it be, always sticking your turtle neck out for others, aren't ya darl."

After explaining what they accomplished that morning, Bazz poured them another ale and simply asked,

"What about the wanted poster, did it have any information on it?"

Purvan, who had been holding on to the parchment, pulled it from his person. He unravelled it and revealed the image of Oophaga, except now, it had been scribbled on. The image of Ooph now had spectacles, a moustache and a goatee. Unfortunately, there was no information on the poster other than WANTED, Oophaga Pumilio and a reward given.

Bazz, looking over at the parchment, let out a sigh, as did the three companions. He then said,

"Didn't they say to report anything to the authorities?"

The party stared at Bazz in a daze.

"Well, they must have a contact if the local boys are involved."

Looking at each other for a moment of realisation, the party got off their stools and hurried out the door. Just then, Minny came back.

"Bazz?" she simply said, her tone relaying her unsaid query.

"Yes, yes, you can go play. I'll get my brother to fill for you tonight." he looked at the bar at the three full mugs of ale, picked one up and took a swig before replying to no one.

"Stone the crows."

A five-minute walk from the Fancy Rabbit was a guard station. Guard stations were small offices where one or two guards would be assigned, if anyone needed to report something. Most other guards would have a patrol route that they would continue to walk during their shift. Minny approached, being the one familiar with the city guard, and left the other two to wait outside.

"Morning, Lieutenant, do you have a moment?"

"Sure, enter, have a seat." He grimaced slightly, realising that Minny would not be able to sit due to her size.

"How can I be of service?"

"I am looking for information regarding this particular situation," Minny explained as she pointed to the same WANTED poster of Ooph on the notice board attached to the wall.

He looked at her, trying to ascertain her intention.

"You work for Barry down the street at the Fancy Rabbit, don't you?"

"That is correct."

"Yes, that's right, you, his security contingent, Whispersea?"

Minorha nodded in recognition.

"Well, for all I know, they are looking for that individual responsible for the murder of a fellow villager."

"Where do they come from?"

"Not really sure, some village in the north, a fair ways off."

"Do you know where they are now, where I can find them?"

"Not exactly, there is no actual location given of the village, and I couldn't really tell you where the little ones that come in are. They just visit the city every two weeks, check with us and do the rounds of local establishments."

"Every two weeks, you say. So they travel home and back again, that seems excessive."

"Oh no, they don't go back to their village. They always leave from the north side of the city and continue to do so. Some of the scouts that go out say there is a small camp out there, which is probably them. They must stay close until they have completed their work."

A look of excited surprise appeared on Minorha's turtle face.

"Well, that is fascinating". She concludes, pausing as she is thinking to herself.

"Is that all?" he asked.

"Yes, thank you, Lieutenant.......?" Her response turned into a query.

"Jonkins," he revealed. "Are you planning to assist the frogs in the investigation?"

Minorha looked at him, trying to conceal her true intentions.

"Of course, Lieutenant."

He looked back at her dubiously.

"Well, just do your civil duty and leave the rest to the authorities, stay out of trouble."

Minorha farewelled Lieutenant Jonkins with a nod and exited the office to join her two companions outside.

As they began to make their way back to Minorha's place, they decided to check in with Stellda at the Hall of Mages. They made their way through the inner city and headed to the large sunstone building with banners hanging down. Two styles of banners fluttered in the breeze; some had the symbol of arcane magic, a swirly fireball and others had the symbol of the Novum Arcanum, called The Arcane Pentacle. It was the symbol that was associated with the god of magic, The Arcanist, Numir. They were usually silver or gold, depending on the level of the mage's skill and worn around the neck on a chain or clasped to the mantle of the robes.

Purvan looked around the square with the Hall and the Great Keep, reminiscing.

"I haven't been here in some time. Doesn't look like much has changed. I will have to come back and do a show sometime."

"Come on, bard, much to do," Minny yelled back.

The party entered the Hall and approached the front desk, the young Elvish woman behind it scribing in a book.

"Hello, we are hoping that we can see our friend who came in yesterday, Stellda Furfoot."

"Just let me look that up", and she took another book, similar to a booking ledger for an inn.

"Here we are, yes. Stellda Furfoot is with Paulos Dejen in room 203. If you go down the main hall here and turn at the second left, continue down that corridor until you reach the room, which will be on the right."

The party thanked her and proceeded down the hall. They turned the corner to the second corridor on the left and made their way to room 203.

KNOCK, KNOCK, KNOCK.

A moment passed, and the door was opened by Stellda, still dressed nicely, but her hair was all a mess.

"What are you lot doing here?" she snapped.

"We came to see how you were progressing," Nectarion responded.

"We are doing shit, of course."

"Come now, dear, we are not here to cause an issue." Purvan moved forward and put on the charm, trying to calm Stellda's mood. She looked at him and gave him a slight stink eye. She looked up,

"Who's the new fella', a turtle?"

"Who you callin' fella?" Minny scorned at Stellda.

"Oh, you're a girl turtle, my apologies."

"Stellda, who is it, my dear? We have much to do here." Behind the door, in the room, stood a male Human of medium height and build, in his thirties, and wearing a full closed-in violet cloth skull cap. His robes were made of green brocade with violet embellishments of runes that run around the edges of the garment, and a violet girdle belt with green coloured runes to match. He also wore a gold chain with clasps on the robe mantle and a badge of office, depicting that he was part of the Novum Arcanum.

"It's all right, Paulos, just some friends about to leave," she yelled into the room behind, then turned back to her friends. "Look, I know you have come to check I am alright, but I'm fine.

The work that my associate and I are doing seems to be extensive and could take more time than I had hoped."

"That pretty much works in our favour because we may have something that could keep us occupied for a while," Purvan explained.

"Nothing too serious, I hope?" She replied.

"Nothing that I can't handle," Minny interjected. Stellda looked up at the towering turtle woman now accompanying the others, a smile of recognition on her face.

"Wait a moment, I have something for you."

Stellda left the door and returned, handing the party a small glass-like orb.

"If you need to contact me, use this. Well then, behave you lot, don't do anything I wouldn't do." She concluded.

"That won't leave much now, then." Nectarion jested.

The party bid her their farewells as she shut the door. The party left the Hall of Mages and began to head back to Minorha's home.

Chapter Six

Minny unlocked the door to her home, and she, Purvan and Nectarion entered the abode. Minny placed her sunhat on the small table with the food that they had brought back with them. Pluteus and Ooph were sitting in the corner of the alcove, vague expressions across their faces. The other three noticed that chunks of Pluteus' cap were missing.

"Looks like your friends couldn't wait for food?"

Purvan and Nectarion looked over at Ooph and Pluteus. The two bore expressions of humour on their faces.

"Yes, in case of an emergency, Pluteus can spare some of his pileus as rations. Unfortunately, there is an amusing side effect. They are both high right now," explained Nectarion.

"Pluteus comes from a village located somewhere north of here. Apparently, his people are made from hallucinogenic properties, some part of their evolution," added Purvan.

Minorha looked on in amusement and then began to set the table for the evening meal. The food from the festival was laid out, and the five companions came together and dined.

It was the last day of the Autumn festival, and the vendors and shopkeepers had packed up as the sun was setting. Organisers and volunteers had begun to clear the streets and remove the festival decorations. The party sat around the small table in Minorha's home, content with the meal they had just finished consuming. Oophaga had begun to come down from their high and was much more coherent now, and Purvan began the conversation.

"So we managed to find out some information about these *associates* of yours", as he looked to Ooph.

"Firstly, they do come from a place somewhere north, no doubt your home. But they have been staying somewhere close to town, rather than travelling the distance back and forth, because they routinely return every two weeks to see if there has been any sighting of their quarry."

Oophaga, still slightly vague, stared at a spot on the table where some food scraps lay.

"Now, this is an issue because if we need to return to this city, which is extremely likely if we are to see Stellda again, then we should deal with this sooner rather than later. What say you, Ooph?"

Ooph sat paused for what seemed like an hour, but after a few moments passed, they responded to the question.

"These people, particularly the one who killed my best friend, have accused me of a crime I didn't commit and then expelled me from my home. I do not wish to return to them, but I feel we can; we should take care of this immediate threat."

"We can set out tomorrow to find this camp of theirs. It is mostly open woodlands, but there is a forest about a day's north of here. I would bet that is where they have established themselves if they were to stay out of sight," Minny added to the conversation.

Ooph looked at their companions with concern in their deep, black eyes, bottomless and yet full of anxiety and hurt.

"My friends, I ask you to aid me in this endeavour, although I am reluctant to do so. This is a personal matter, and I understand if I must attend to it on my own."

The other three and Minorha, now also a companion, looked at Oophaga and each placed a hand on their back, and Pluteus remarked.

"We will help you, Ooph, you are our friend and we have come to care for you."

A small drop of water appeared in the corner of one of Ooph's eyes, and the party of five all gathered in for a hug. Minny almost encompassed all of them in her large turtle arms.

The next morning, the party arose from their slumber and decided to get an early start by picking up supplies. Pluteus was showing off his greatsaff, which he had been working on for weeks, enhancing its ability and power based on the instructions he had found in the Book of Tyfar, which was gifted to him by Stellda.

After a quick run to the equipment store and local apocrypha, the party grabbed a quick bite at the Fancy Rabbit, said goodbye to Bazz, and began their trek north.

The journey north was relatively easy and pleasant. The open plain with trees spread sparsely across it, the Autumn sun's warmth made it all the more enjoyable in the coolness, and yet there was a stillness on the companions, an air of thickness. No one spoke; they simply continued north. Ooph's thoughts weighed heavily on their mind. What would they do when they finally come face-to-face with their accuser? Would they seek absolute vengeance or let him go as an act of mercy? It seemed it continued to come back to vengeance.

"Let the pond scum bleed." Ooph thought to themself.

The day passed, from morning to midday. The party stopped for a short break and a light meal before continuing. The afternoon was steadily moving towards sunset, and the temperature was dropping from a nice warmth to an afternoon chill. The party could see the tree line of the forest that Minny had mentioned.

Just as the sun kissed the treetops to the west, the party reached the forest's edge. They paused for a moment, surveying the scene and making sure to be cautious before proceeding. The others all looked at Ooph.

"Are you sure about this?" Nectarion asked.

Ooph stood stationary for a moment before they gripped the hilt of their sword and, with determination and a newfound confidence, led the party into the forest.

The party had only ventured a short way when they could hear chatter and even croaking. They slowly moved through the trees, remaining as quiet as possible, each step as soft as the last. There, through the trees in a small clearing, sat six Ribbets, lounging around a campfire. Each had their bedroll set up, and they were unarmed; their weapons lay on the ground next to them. They were enjoying the evening meal while conversing in their native tongue. Ooph and Purvan, who could understand the language of Ribbets, listened closely.

"What are they saying?" Nectarion inquired.

The others all turned to him, pressing their index finger to their mouths, indicating to be quiet. After a few moments of listening, Ooph turned to their companions.

"They are just making idle chit-chat, nothing important."
Purvan's expression indicated that he concurred.

"That one there, that is the leader, Anthrax Vossen, who murdered my best friend." Ooph pointed out a particular Ribbet, sitting just off to the side and enjoying his meal in solitude while looking on at his comrades in amusement. Purvan and Minny could recognise him from the Fancy Rabbit, where they saw him two nights ago. Minny turned to her friends and asked.

"Okay. What's the plan?"

They all turned to Purvan, who rolled his eyes.

"Okay, I'll come up with the plan. They are all unsuspecting at the moment; they most likely don't believe anyone would approach them out here. We have two options: we can kill them outright, or we can subdue them and get information."

Ooph looked at Purvan. "There is no need for questions; they are bastards and deserve to die."

The party looked at Ooph with concern as they saw anger in their eyes.

"Understandable. This is your headache, Ooph, so we will defer to your advice," advised Purvan.

"We should surround the camp, each mark one of them, and when a signal is given, we move in quickly and dispatch them. Running them through without hesitation, and it will be all over."

Minny looked on in excitement that she might actually get to bash something, and Pluteus was just happy to help. Purvan and Nectarion had reservations but hid them well from the others. The party began to move slowly, staying hidden in the trees while encircling the small clearing. Just before they parted, Purvan turned to Nectarion and said,

"I understand Ooph is hurt and wants to avenge the death of her friend, but I feel there is more to this than a simple murder."

"I agree, some elements are missing from Ooph's account that give me pause. What do you suggest we do, though, once we begin? Ooph is set on killing these individuals"

"True, some of them will most likely meet their end, but if we can spare one or two, especially the ring-leader, then it might be enough, and Ooph will just have to understand."

Necatrion nodded in agreement, and the two separated and got into position.

The camp of Ribbets was laughing, eating and drinking merrily, and they remained oblivious as five individuals slowly surrounded them. As before every battle, there was a stillness in the air.

A pinkish blur leapt from the trees and made the first attack against one of the unsuspecting campers. From the other side of the clearing, a large bumblebee emerged, and Nectarion wasted no time as a wave of arcane energy shot from one of his four hands and pushed back the Ribbet known as Anthrax. Anthrax, who managed to stand as Ooph sprang into action, was pushed back, moving him closer into Ooph's range.

From the tree line, an icy spike soared through the air and hit its mark; the sheer force of it pierced one of the two dark-skinned Ribbets. The wound was so large it left a substantial hole in the small individual as it now lay in a puddle of its blood and entrails.

Minorha appeared next and charged at the other dark-skinned Ribbet and his yellow comrade. In her hand, a mace

90

that looked more like a small tree that was ripped out by the roots and now functioned as Minny's weapon. She swung it and crushed it into the yellow Ribbet's head; it too now lay on the ground in a pool of goop, its eyeballs sunken back and its brains spilled from its mouth. She then turned to the dark-skinned Ribbet and, using the butt of her weapon, knocked him unconscious.

Ooph, now on Anthrax's position, cast Viscious Entangle on him. Vines shot up from the soil and attempted to grapple him, but his Ribbet reflexes were too quick as he hopped from the spot out of danger.

Nectarion closed in on Anthrax from the other side, casting another spell in an attempt to subdue the Ribbet before Oophaga could kill him.

Pluteus now entered the clearing and made for another one of the Ribbets, a green-skinned one. Plutues cast a spell at the Ribbet, and the arcane power missed the small frog-folk as it moved quickly to dodge the attack. It then turned to Pluteus, a wide grin across its large frog face and pulled a dagger from its belt, although for him it could have been a shortsword. It lunged at Pluteus's large mushroom form and penetrated him, only to discover that all he had accomplished was getting his weapon tangled up in Pluteus's robes, which were practically made from the same substance as his mushroom body. A robe full of holes, the dagger now hung there, like it was stuck in cobwebs.

From across the campsite, a crimson-skinned Ribbet finally picked up his bow and nocked an arrow, aiming it directly at Oophaga. As the Ribbet released the arrow, Minny, standing not but five feet from the Ribbet, moved quickly in front of the shot.

91

Her strong turtle shell rejected the arrow's damage, and it fell to the ground.

Pluteus, still engaged with the green-skinned Ribbet, attempted another spell attack and again, the agile frog leapt around the towering mushroom. The crimson-skinned Ribbet, frustrated with what would have been an epic shot, moved around the lumbering Galapa and fired another arrow at Oophaga. Anthrax now attempted to close in on Ooph as well, making an unsuccessful attack with his bow.

Nectarion saw his opportunity and approached Anthrax from behind while he was engaged with Ooph and, with the butt of his axe, knocked the Ribbet unconscious. The blue-skinned Ribbet was now lying in a heap on the ground as if he were sound asleep.

Finally, standing over them, Minny intimidated the remaining Ribbets, forcing them to lay down their arms and surrender. So successful was she that one dropped everything and fled the campsite into the forest. The rustling of leaves could be heard for a short moment until there was silence. He had leapt his way out of the situation.

The dark-skinned, green-skinned and the blue-skinned Anthrax are all brought together, and Minny tied them up with some rope. So much of it was there that the only visible parts of their bodies were their frog heads, popping out of the top of the coiled bindings. The only conscious Ribbet was the green-skinned individual.

The party, now surrounding these three restrained Ribbets, stand over the small folk. Minorha's towering presence, still very intimidating. Nectarion stepped right up to the green-skinned Ribbet.

"You will answer our questions, or you will die."

"We don't need to ask questions; they *do* need to die, though." The blade of Ooph's broadsword pointed at the Ribbet as they began to come close. Purvan moved forward and placed his hand on their shoulder, holding them back slightly and trying to calm them. He looked at Nectarion to proceed.

"Tell us why you pursue our associate?"

"Our task here was to simply track down the murderer."

"How do you know she is responsible?"

"We were told so by our commander, he was a witness to it," and the green-skinned Ribbet motioned his eyes to the blue-skinned Ribbet that is Anthrax.

"Were there any other witnesses?" injected Purvan.

"No, just the commander."

"What else do you know?"

"Nothing, that is all I have been made aware of."

Minny moved her stance slightly, covering the Ribbet in darkness as she stood in the way of the firelight. The green-skinned Ribbet became more anxious.

"I swear, it is all I know. The commander would know more."

Nectarion looked over at the unconscious Anthrax and placed his hand on the Ribbet's forehead. A slight arcane glow emanated from his hand, and Anthrax began to stir, waking, somewhat groggy from the concussion he now had from the fight moments ago.

Oophaga tried to move, but Purvan maintained his grip on their shoulder.

"You are Anthrax?" continued Nectarion.

He looked about the scene groggily before looking at the giant bumblebee.

"I am he. What is the meaning of this?" he responded, becoming quite aware of Oophaga's proximity with their sword tightly gripped in their hand. His energy shifted from demanding to anxious.

"Answer the questions and you may yet walk away from this," Nectarion informed.

"We want to know, did our friend here commit the murder you say they are responsible for. They tell us a different story, stating they are innocent."

"She is far from innocent."

"I grow tired of these silly games. I want answers, you little blue fuck." Nectarion's voice rose, and he took his Hallowed axe and placed the blade's edge right under Anthrax's vocal sack. His anxious persona escalated to fear and distress as the sharpness of the blade could be felt on his skin.

"Okay, okay, I'll tell you, just don't kill me." he looked at Nectarion and then at Ooph as they were ready to make a lunge for him. The confident commander was now a pathetic, snivelling wreck.

"My father ordered me to track her down and end her, to prevent her from revealing the truth."

"So who murdered Oophaga's friend?" Purvan inquired.

He looked at the party, the edge of Nectarion's axe moved but a millimetre, and he could feel the additional pressure applied.

"It was I who killed her."

"Why? What did she do?"

94

" She had discovered my father." Anthrax paused and gulped. "She discovered my father communing with a dark entity, a demon."

"Who, which demon?"

Anthrax, still extremely terrified that his throat would be slit if he moved or more pressure was applied, was somewhat reluctant to answer but thought better of it.

"He is known as the First Lieutenant of the Morning Star. His name is Azazel."

The party all looked at each other to see if anyone had an inkling of this name. Plutues then responded.

"I know that name. I read about it in my early training. A scroll detailing a particular demon, the one he mentioned, Azazel. He is meant to be the right hand of a devil referred to as the Morning Star. He is also supposed to be the father of the first Infernis."

"What the hell does that all mean?" Minny asked.

"I don't know, the scroll was a single parchment of information, and I paid it no attention in the end because I've not met anyone who has heard much about this Azazel or demons and devils for that matter."

The party relaxed a little after this explanation, and Nectarion removed his axe from Anthrax's throat. Purvan looked at Ooph and said,

"Do you now have resolve?"

"Not quite." They moved like a flash at Anthrax with their sword. He could see their blade swing overhead, and he closed his eyes in anticipation of the strike. But nothing happened, death did not come, and he opened his eyes slightly to notice the blade stopped just before his face.

"I want you gone, go home and tell them, tell your father to leave me alone. Lie if you have to, I don't care, just stop coming after me. I will not be coming home," They dropped their sword to the ground. The rest of the party looked on in surprise, but also relief that Ooph didn't succumb to revenge.

"Do you agree to these terms?" Nectarion asked.

Anthrax looked up and, without saying a word, nodded his head vigorously in agreement, anxious to be released and live. Minny untied the three Ribbets and gave them a slight shove to leave. Anthrax and the green-skinned Ribbet collected the unconscious friend and carried him from the camp immediately, leaving all their belongings behind.

Once they had left and the party was comfortable with the distance they had gone, no longer hearing the rustling of leaves from the dragging Ribbet's feet, the party decided to take a few benefits and looted the camp, picking up a few general supplies and even a few specialty items. Purvan approached Oophaga as they had not participated in the looting and sat down beside them.

"Are you okay?" he asked, concerned.

"I just......... I am just happy that that is over. Hopefully, I will not have to face that issue again."

"So you can never go home again, can you accept that decision?"

"Yes, my people did not believe me and my father, a member of the council, did nothing. It was like he didn't even care." They sat next to Purvan, and a moment of silence had fallen over the two as they processed the incident. He placed his hand on their shoulder once more in comfort, and the two exchanged glances with a look of acceptance. Then Purvan broke the silence.

"Why did he refer to you as *'she'*? I thought you were non-binary?"

"I am; he just has no respect."

After the party had had a good scrounge and collected what they wanted, they decided to move and not linger. They began the trek back to Westhold. The sun was well set, but it was still early evening, probably 'dinner time'. The party estimated they should be back at Westhold by midnight. Being the last day of the month, the moon had reached its nadir. The glow of the moon, named Dilmiri, was dull but still managed to provide a dim light, a soft blanket of stars behind it. To the south, a small bright reddish-orange star could be seen. The Ubius star takes a thousand years to complete its orbital journey, reaching its zenith at the beginning of a new age. It was currently aligned with the south pole of the realm, and soon, the decade of deep cold will occur.

The party began to feel the effects of a long day as they reached almost eighteen hours without a proper rest. They finally made it back to Westhold and headed straight to Minorha's home. Ooph and Necatrion crashed instantly as sleep took them. Pluteus took a bit before he reached deep sleep. Purvan and Minny lay close to each other, and he briefly said that they would make a proper plan when the sun rises, and the two also found sleep.

The party rose in the morning. The hour was not late, but the sun had definitely made its first hours of climb. There was a completely different air about the five of them, as if yesterday

97

didn't happen. They all seemed to be in a generally good mood, their spirits high.

"So what do we want to do today?" Pluteus asked.

"Is there anything we can do?" added Minny. "I mean, were you on some kind of mission with your friend at the Hall of Mages?"

"Yeah, but we are currently in an interlude. We could simply stay in town and enjoy the relaxation until something comes about." Purvan added.

"Why don't we go out and see what is happening. Do a bit of shopping and maybe get something to eat," the cheerful and sweet voice of Ophaga broke into the conversation.

The party all looked at one another and agreed.

Using some of the loot they obtained from the Ribbet's camp, the party picked up a few more supplies. Nectarion traded in his Hallowed axe and shield for some awesome upgrades. He then used the stone they found at the Ribbet's camp and bound it to his new weapon.

"A greatstone it is called", Pluteus explained, "with the ability to increase the power of your weapon."

Nectarion was ecstatic and held his axe in two hands, curled his bee-like mouth up and growled like a hardened warrior. Minorha just looked on in amusement.

Afterwards, as the morning approached midday, the party headed to the Fancy Rabbit for a late breakfast, or perhaps an early lunch. As they sat and ate their meal, three large covered wagons appeared out the front. What seemed to be a dozen or so individuals accompanied the caravan. One of them, a male Human with short grey hair and basic blue and green cotton clothes, entered the tavern and talked to Bazz behind the bar.

The party can hear the conversation; his company had arrived to pick up the barrels of ale they had ordered. Bazz yelled out to his brother in the back, and the two began to bring out eight large barrels of 'Rabbit's Foot' ale, the Fancy Rabbits' brand of ale that Bazz and his brother brewed on the premises.

"What is all the commotion?" Purvan asked as he looked at Minorha.

"That's the excavation caravan. They come into town every few months, pick up supplies and head out across the Edron Plains to an excavation site."

"What excavation site? I've never heard of one out there." Nectarion responded in incredulous surprise.

"The site is of an old ruined city that existed during the Forgotten Millenia; it was only discovered about a hundred and fifty years ago," added Minorha.

"Well, why don't we head out there with them, take a look at some history? It's not like we have any immediate plans."

The party looked intrigued and hopped up from the table and approached the man who was handing the payment to Bazz.

In that moment, the party could see that all three wagons were fully loaded with supplies, tools and equipment, food and now the ale. There were at least two individuals in each of the driver's seats, and the rest sat on planks of wood bolted to the side of the wagons with iron brackets.

"Greetings, my name is Nectarion. My companions and I are interested in joining your caravan to the excavation site."

"I'm sorry, friend, but I can't afford to employ anyone else." He pointed his thumb over his shoulder at the others with the wagons.

"I've already got this lot on the books to deal with."

"My apologies, good sir…"

"Stan," the man interjected.

"Stan. We would not require any form of employment or payment. We are simply interested in seeing the ruins. We are intrigued. But if you require any additional aid, my friends and I would be happy to assist."

Stan looked at the party and noticed they were not average citizens or even commoners. He could tell they were adventurers. An occupation that was rarely taken up lightly, and their numbers were said to be well under a hundred across all of Edron. He responded to the offer.

"Alright, I could use a group of individuals such as yourself, BUT, it's volunteer work only, no pay and when you get there, don't get in the way of the archaeologists, probably best if you don't wander around without supervision, probably best if you don't wander at all."

Nectarion put out one of his four hands, and Stan slapped it in accordance to signify that a verbal contract had been completed.

Stan turned to the caravan and yelled to get the wagon train moving. Most of the smaller members of the party join the others on the bench seats, but Minorha and Pluteus have to walk. Nectarion decided to take to the sky about twenty feet above the top of the wagon.

The wagon train slowly navigated the streets of Westhold and made the perimeter, continuing out of the city and out onto the

Edron Plains. It will spend the next few weeks travelling through the farmlands of Edron before reaching its destination. With the party now finding more purpose as they continue their journey through the realm, what wonders will they encounter next?

Chapter Seven

The party stood silently in the large canvas tent. Before them, a large wooden table with a plain white tablecloth stood in the centre, covered in various items such as parchment, quill and ink, a magnifying glass, a mug half full with what looks to be coffee or tea and a few tomes, one of which is open to a page showing script of an old runic dialect.

Set against the tent wall, on one side was a bookcase, half filled with other tomes, and on the other, there was a shelf with different objects and artifacts from the dig site. Against the back wall was another table with pieces of stone, decorated with runes and tools for cleaning artifacts.

Standing across the table from the party was a six-and-a-half-foot blue Drakonan, R'kar, the main foreman of the Deimos dig site. Wearing a three-quarter-length, thin leather tunic with a tight leather belt wrapped around his waist. He had two small pouches on his belt with what looked like tools used for archaeology. His back was turned to the party as he stared off into the corner of the tent.

Deimos is the name of the city that the archaeologists have unearthed here. It was discovered about one hundred and forty-five years ago. Originally a part of a larger kingdom known as Hof'Angar. It has a sister city to the northeast called Phobos, which was only discovered eighty-nine years ago.

The party arrived two days ago, after spending a week and a half crossing the Edron plains, through the farmlands with the caravan of supplies and equipment. Since their arrival, they have helped Stan, the caravan leader, unload and distribute the goods. The party was even allowed to enter the surface areas of the dig site to do so, but was given strict instructions not to venture into the subterranean areas.

The party had met with R'kar on the first day they arrived and expressed their interest in exploring the ruins and perhaps helping with some of the more delicate projects.

As R'kar turned to face the party, he responded,

"I have already stated that it would be unwise to grant you access to the subterranean areas without proper experience in how to handle an emergency. The ruins in some areas are quite delicate, and a cave-in could occur at any time, and I am not willing to risk the lives of some would-be heroes, looking to make a name for themselves."

The party remained silent for a moment, then a noise of the tent flapping came from behind them. An Elf entered, tall, with long blonde hair done up in a large bun and full of dust. He was wearing light coloured, earth-toned cotton robes. On his leather belt was a toolkit with a brush and a rowel.

"Gantar, how can I be of assistance?"

"Just dropping off that report on the new find yesterday."

The Elf, Gantar, hands R'kar a handful of parchment rolled up in leather. He unravelled it and looked over Gantar's notes.

"Have you discovered any theories on how to enter the next chamber?"

"Not as yet. We are still working on them."

R'kar looked at the party with intrigue and then placed the parchment on his desk.

"You have been eager to help. If you can work out this particular conundrum, I will consider giving you access to the lower levels, under supervision, of course."

Before them on the desk lay sketches of a chamber. One depicted a stone wall with runic script, another with various images of handprints. Gantar stepped forward.

"That there, is the wall which we believe is actually a door. We know that there is another space on the other side. See here, this space in the wall, which is a perfect square. We know that these tiles go into the wall, but we are unsure of the combination."

"Have you tried different combinations already? Ooph inquired.

"We have created some ideas, but we have not put any into practice. We do not wish to go shoving the tiles into the wall all willy-nilly in case we trigger something dangerous."

Pluteus looked at the other sketch of the wall with runes.

"This writing, I've not seen it before. Have you been able to translate it?"

"Interesting, I have not come across anything like it either," Purvan added.

"We know they are runic in nature, but we have never seen this dialect. Most of the runes in the city are of Elvish or Dwarven origin. This is a completely undiscovered dialect. It could even predate all other known dialects."

The party turned to the sketches of the tiles. Nectarion folded the parchment so that the edge of the tile sketch aligned with the edge of the parchment. The others saw what he was attempting and aided him. They could then see that the images of the handprints must align in some way, now to discover the combination.

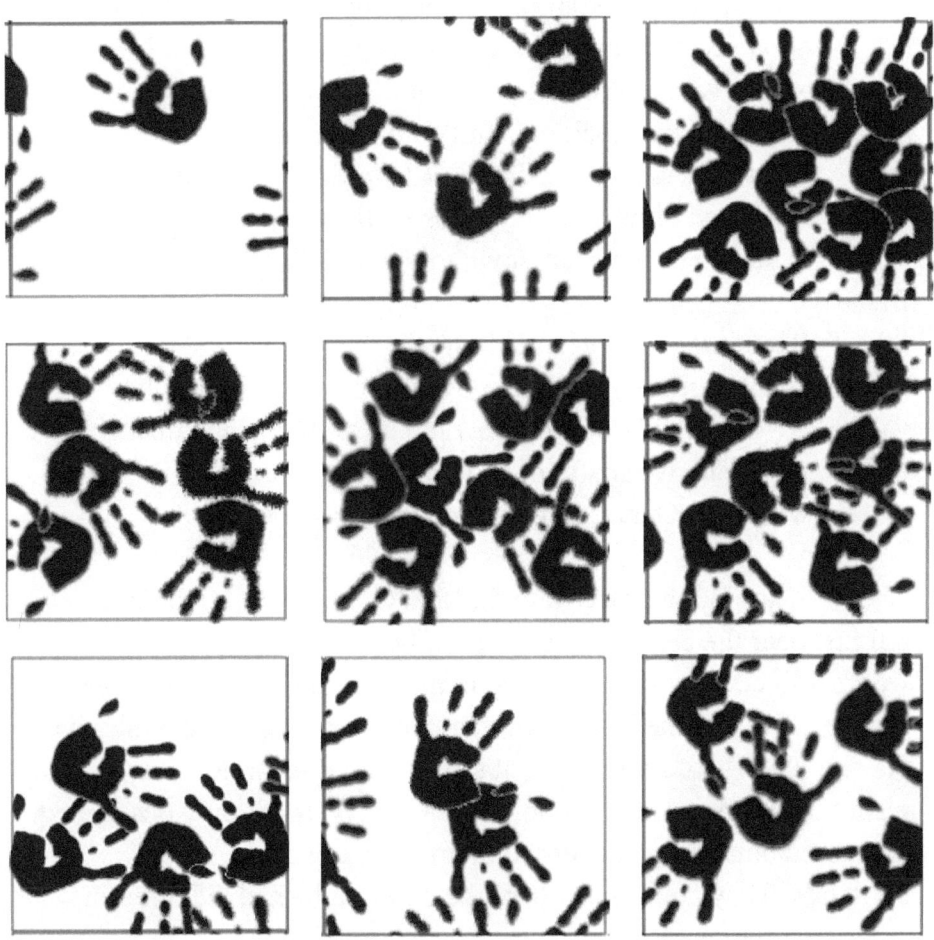

The party spent some time arranging the tiles in various patterns and combinations, with Gantar and R'kar looking over their shoulders and adding their own ideas in. Eventually, the companions discovered a combination that R'kar and Gantar felt might be acceptable to attempt. Oophaga pointed out the pattern.

"You see, the square in this sketch indicates that it is a three-by-three square. You place the nine tiles in this arrangement, and you will find that each row and column equals fifteen."

"You're absolutely brilliant. Why didn't I see this before?" Gantar expressed himself with joyous realisation.

"Maybe you've been down in that hole too long, my friend?"

"Nonsense, I love being in holes."

"Well, I guess you have proven to me that you can be valuable. I will allow you to follow me down to the chamber. Gantar, go ahead, we shall not be long behind you."

With that, Gantar left the tent.

R'kar led the party into the site, taking them up the grassy hill just near the campsite made up of hundreds of tents, where the workers lived. Dirt paths leading in different directions made their way to the top of the hill. From there, looking down into a massive dig site with ruined structures, it stretched out for miles. It was a giant hole in the ground, almost like a quarry, but it only descended about one hundred and fifty feet before the top of the first buildings. They could see where the other paths had led, granting access to other areas.

Stairs carved into the hard dirt of the dig site allow access down into the hole. The party saw the workers going about their duties, digging and clearing away dirt and stone. Archaeologists were completely focused on the finer particulars, trying to clear the dirt away from various sections, some statues, and others' writings.

The party ventured down into the ruins of this ancient city. There were Elves, Dwarves, Humans, and Halflings working in various parts of the ruins. They passed a few Drakona and even a few small groups of Goblins.

The city ruins were extensive, and the further down they went, the more scarce the light became; lit torches and some light stones provided light this far down.

Finally, after half an hour, the group had reached the chamber where Gantar awaited them. He had already begun to place the tiles into the slots on the wall, and so far, they were matching up nicely. Each step he proceeded cautiously, ensuring that nothing in the chamber had been triggered that could cause a cave-in or worse.

"I am almost done, just two tiles left," Gantar informed out loud.

"Why don't you just hurry up and put them in? We're getting anxious." Nectarion burst out with annoyance.

"Because, willy-nilly." Gantar replied, looking at R'kar, "Remember what happened to Jespon?"

R'kar nodded with agreement.

"What happened to Jespon?" queried Purvan.

"Willy-nilly." Gantar and R'kar responded in unison.

Gantar eventually placed the final tile in the last slot, and there was a moment of silence.

A loud clonk noise filled and echoed through the chamber. Another, and the wall began to part down the middle, the sound of the large stone pieces moving, the passageway opening. The doors stopped, and the stirred dust began to float down to the ground. Before the group was a dark opening, cool air with a bite to it rushed out. An empty, black void with a spine-chilling wind lay before them.

"Gantar, I want you to stay here, in case we need you to seek help. I am going to take our adventurers here to do some preliminary exploration."

"Yes, sir."

R'kar picked up a torch, and the party grabbed a couple of extra torches as they entered the dark chamber.

As they entered the next chamber, they noticed that it descended into darkness. The party and R'kar made their way down the worn stone stairs that crumbled slightly under their footsteps; the walls were rough and hewn, and it seemed the passage was carved to grant access.

After about twenty minutes in the dark, narrow stairwell, the companions came out into an open area of ruins. It looked like it used to be a main public area, a place where people would gather; the remains of various buildings had been reduced to practically nothing after centuries of decay. The city architecture was extremely layered, as the ruins closer to the surface were as extensive as they were down here, almost like two separate cities joined together.

Large columns that formed thoroughways extended into the cavern roof above, and in between sat the remains of buildings. Every five or six buildings, there was a cross-section as one thoroughway intersected the other.

The group, led by R'kar, slowly wandered around, taking in the sight. There was natural light coming from the cavern roof above, but it was difficult to see where it originated. As light shone in, it hit a large, silvery metal disc, which in turn reflected and hit another. About a dozen discs could be seen in the local proximity, and they provided the ruins with light.

R'kar could hardly believe what he was seeing as he was immensely distracted by the ruins. He noticed a few runes carved into the decaying buildings, but it was the same dialect that hadn't yet been translated.

The group finally wandered into the centre of a massive city courtyard. There stood a large arched structure, about twelve feet tall and eight feet wide. It would have most likely been a courtyard arch, with the exception that it had been bricked up, and no one could pass through it. Around the haunch, as the learned

Purvan referred to the arching section, the stones had runes carved into them, as did the keystone at the top. R'kar approached it and removed a pair of loupe spectacles and studied the archway.

"Fascinating," he said, aloud to himself. "Very interesting".

"What, What is? Is it a magical archway?" Nectarion eagerly questioned.

"It might quite possibly be."

Ooph moved towards the arch and placed one of their forelimbs on the arch. They closed their eyes, and a slight glow engulfed them.

"What is it, Ooph? Can you sense anything?"

Purvan approached now and began his own sense of the object.

"I can sense something as well. An arcane energy."

"I am sensing something more of a divine nature."

The group took a moment and stood back, looking at this simple stone arch that somehow contained an energy of arcane and divine natures. The party knew that something like this was

somewhat paradoxical, as the two types of energy are opposites of one another.

"Maybe we could bash it down?" suggested Minny, and before anyone could respond, she charged towards the stone wall in the centre of the arch. Minny hit the wall hard and dropped to the ground like a rag doll.

"The wall wasn't even that thick; that should have worked," she claimed, as she picked herself up.

At just that moment, the ground shook with a tremor, and the ruins crumbled slightly.

"It might be that these ruins aren't entirely stable down here." R'kar speculated, and the party looked at him with amusement at the confounded obviousness of his comment before turning back to the arch.

"There is definitely something about this arch that needs further study, but for now, perhaps we should press on," motioned R'kar as he turned and began to walk further into the ruins, the party following close behind.

The companions continued exploring, and the ruins began to show severe structural compromises as even the stone ground began to crumble away. As the party explored this new area, they found many wonderful statues of people in strange poses. Some of them showed confounding expressions, while others showed shock and fear.

The party stopped suddenly as they reached an edge; a massive drop lay before them. Around the edge, seven large crystal formations, each the size of an average humanoid, were embedded into the precipice of the gapping hole, each a different colour:

yellow, orange, green, blue, epsilon, red and white. The hole looked to be sixty feet wide, and as they looked down, there seemed to be a soft reddish-yellow glow quite a fair way down.

"Now that's a hole, and I should know," Purvan said aloud.

"This is amazing, beyond anything I could have imagined." R'kar was ecstatically expressing his thoughts. "We have spent years looking for some significant find; we would have been happy with a library, a well of knowledge from our past, but this…"

The sound of rubble falling could be heard just off to the side of the hole behind them.

"Did you hear that?" asked Nectarion. No one responded.

Ooph, then noticed that there were walkways around the side of the hole, what remains of the street that once passed through here. They headed off to the right in an attempt to reach the far side. Purvan noticed and followed behind them. As they approached, the integrity of the stone failed and crumbled apart, falling into the hole towards the glow at the bottom. Ooph jumped back on their frog legs, and Purvan caught them.

"That was a close one," declared Ooph.

Ooph and Purvan returned to where the rest of the party stood and decided to try the other side; this time, they all went. As they did, Nectarion picked up Purvan to help cross over the edge, and as they passed an old, decayed building, one of many that occupied this area, a creature the party had never seen before emerged from the shadow.

A large serpent-like creature with a human torso came forth, its tail stretching over fifteen feet. Its torso extruded four arms, and upon its head, it had snakes for hair. Its tail coiled around as it slithered toward the party. It screeched at them, the

112

noise pierced their ears as it echoed through the subterranean chasm.

"What the hell is that?"

R'kar, in absolute fear, ran and jumped behind a fallen pillar. The party, now surrounding the creature, took a defensive stance. They knew that this creature wished to harm them, but they must be cautious, standing so close to the massive opening in the ground.

"Move me closer," Purvan commanded as he looked up at Nectarion. The Apis-fae, with his comrade in his hands, flew towards the creature, and as he did, Purvan cast Wild Flame, and a stream of fire hit the creature, but it showed no effect.

The creature turned to its attacker and revealed a weapon, a golden short bow adorned with spikes. It pointed the weapon at Purvan and nocked an elaborate-looking arrow in it, and let it loose. It wooshed through the air over the short distance, hitting Purvan. Seriously injured, Nectarion placed Purvan down on the ground. Purvan was now glowing bright with light.

"The arrows have magical properties; be careful!" Nectarion yelled to his friends.

The creature fired a second arrow, and Nectarion used his shield to deflect it. Standing up, Nectarion cast his spell, Bolt Beacon, a bright light streamed toward the creature, hitting it and making it vulnerable.

The creature looked Nectarion dead in the eyes, and an arcane flash washed over the creature's own. Nectarion, standing his ground, began to feel a tightness in his chest, but for some reason it momentarily passed. Seemingly aggravated, the creature now turned its gaze to the small frog-like creature. Nocking

113

another arrow with its short bow, it fired a deadly shot at Oophaga. In an instant, the large Galapa that is Minorha stepped in front of the shot and took the arrow instead, protruding from her leg, and she began to glow as bright as Purvan.

The creature again stared dead into Minny's eyes; she felt something in her chest tighten; something was happening. She looked down at her chest and noticed something - it was turning to stone. In this instant, the party looked on in horror as they realised that the statues they had passed earlier were most likely victims of this creature.

Ooph moved to make an attack and cast Cinder Grasp, engulfing the creature in flames. As the creature's serpent-like body flailed in agony, Ooph turned to Minny to see if they could stave off the transformation.

Nectarion swung his axe at the creature, cleaving a massive wound across its tail, its hair of snakes bit at him, and he brought his axe up for a second swing, taking off one of the creature's arms. The creature, engulfed in flame and agony, continued to thrash around. Ooph could see that each time Nectarion hit the creature, the transformation in Minny slowed but didn't stop. Taking a chance, they left Minny's side and powered toward the creature, taking a massive frog leap while it was facing away. Ooph swung their massive broadsword and decapitated the vile entity.

At that moment, the transformation to stone halted and dissipated, and the tight feeling in Minny's chest subsided. She stood up and collected herself, then began to make her way over to her friends. Nectarion was now by Purvan's side, using his healing gifts to help him and removing the arrow from his shoulder.

"Thank you, my friend, I have never felt such pain before, but I am glad you were here," Purvan gratefully thanked Nectraion as he got to his feet.

"Perhaps you should invest in something a little tougher than silk," the two laughed in unison. The party now saw the creature on the ground, still flaming but mostly burnt to a crispy snake corpse. R'kar emerged from his haven of safety, and at his feet was the head of the creature. He kicked it toward the party in disgust.

"WHOA, be careful with that, we don't know if it's still active," yelled the party.

"What is it?"

"We're not exactly sure, but we have a fair idea it is what created all those statues we saw," explained Oophaga.

"I felt something happening when it looked into my eyes, that's when I could see my body turning to stone," added Minny.

"So how come you're still moving?"

"Because we killed the creature before the transformation completed." Ooph continued.

"So what about the others?" R'kar asked as he turned to look in the direction of the statues. The party joined in looking in the same direction, but nothing stirred.

Nectarion and Purvan decided to take the head as it might prove useful, or perhaps it could be studied. The ability to turn something to stone was not unheard of, but this particular creature had never been documented. They found an old piece of cloth and threw it over their heads, then carefully tied some rope around it and picked it up.

Ooph, Minny and Pluteus investigated the burnt body and discovered it was wearing a chain shirt that had not been affected by the fire. Carefully, they removed the chain shirt, the body still quite fresh, the charred outer layer of scales fell to the ground, and the cooked snake meat became exposed. The three of them looked at the meat and then each other, and in a silent acknowledgement, they didn't take the meat.

"Look what we picked up," Pluteus announced to the others.

Purvan, Nectarion and R'kar all look at the chain shirt with eagerness.

"Where did you find that?" queried R'kar

"On the snake monster," responded Minny. Purvan placed his hand on it, not a scratch or a char mark on it; it was in pristine condition.

"I can sense some kind of arcane energy bound to this item. Perhaps if we take it to an expert mage, they may be able to tell us what its properties exactly are."

"You can't remove artifacts from the dig site without strict permission."

The party all stared at R'kar.

"And I permit you. It can be my way of saying thank you. If you had not been here, I or anyone could have been killed. We have been working on this site for over a century and never had to deal with anything ike this."

"Perhaps it would be prudent to hire some individuals of such skill to assist you in further exploration of this discovery," recommended Minny.

"Yes, I would strongly agree. But for now, it might be best if we return to the surface with what new information we have and put together a bigger team. There is much here to study."

The party moved away from the gaping maw in the ground and cautiously returned the way they came. Passing the statues they came across before, R'kar explained that they would research ways that could possibly reverse the effect of these poor souls. They returned past the arch and ascended the dark, narrow stairwell that exited at the top into the chamber where they met with Gantar. R'kar explained everything he had seen with eagerness and dramatic flair, especially the parts where the party acted valiantly.

Returning to R'kar's tent, he asked Gantar to put together a team of the best and to arm them with any possible tool or weapon. He then turned to the companions standing there, still recovering somewhat from their injuries.

"If you have had your fill of archeology, there might be something else you can do for me?"

"What service can we now provide?"

"Take this scroll requesting the Lord Governor to assign soldiers to the dig site for protection. Obo in Goshan is more acquainted with the work here than Athalia in Westhold."

"We will leave on the morrow if that is acceptable."

R'kar looked at the party and, with a smirk of recognition on his face, he agreed.

Chapter Eight

After spending the past week in Goshan, the party had become a little restless. Spending time out in the world, adventuring, had created an imbalance in their desires. They no longer felt they could sit still. They had left the dig site of Deimos two weeks ago and returned to the city to deliver a scroll to the Lord Governor from R'kar, the head foreman of the dig site. A new area of the city, deep underground, had been discovered, and it posed some interesting yet dangerous obstacles.

After delivering the scroll to Lord Governor Obo, he congratulated the party for their deeds since their departure. The party visited the Hall of Mages and met an Elf named Siriana of the Silver Mages within the Novum Arcanum. She helped the companions identify the chain shirt they found at Deimos. She explained that it had an incredible, magical aura about it and could even be considered a legendary item. Items long ago lost that held great powers and abilities, used and wielded by the greatest heroes of the time, or it could be just another ordinary magical item.

Ooph researched tomes about plant life with healing properties and began compiling a compendium of their own to take back out. Nectarion had rarely been seen as he looked for information and leads relating to the death of his former queen.

Purvan opened his home to his friends, a penthouse within the inner section of the city, gifted to him by the Lord Governor. It has been quiet except for Siriana, who has come to visit Purvan every night since they met.

On the seventh evening back in Goshan, the majority of the companions were sitting around the dining table, reviewing information and determining their next course of action. Siriana was there, and Nectarion had just returned from his continuing investigation. He sat down in an armchair nearby and pulled a small book from his pack. Opening it, he began to quietly write within it.

Purvan, Pluteus and Siriana sat at the table. K.D.'s journal was out and open, a couple of maps that had been furled out and weighed down, one of which Minorha had provided from her days in the Syndicate. It is forbidden to share such information; the Tearrapin Syndicate's trade rules state that no one outside the Syndicate is allowed to benefit from their business. Siriana had also provided some tomes from the Hall of Mages, searching for information on the location of a library with extensive knowledge. It could potentially help the group in relation to the archway they found in the ruins, among other things.

"Look here, this map cuts off before the Redwood Forest, but we are aware that there is another kingdom to the west," explained Pluteus, pointing to the map Minny provided.

"If we can find passage on a ship, we can sail north to Stone Shell Harbour. Then travel to here, where I have heard talk of a library that could be the one Siriana mentioned." Minny showed the route they could take on the map and pointed to the location marked *'Fractured Anvil'*.

"But can we arrange passage on a ship? Doesn't the Syndicate restrict travel to overseas locations?" queried Purvan.

"It's true, it would be difficult to secure passage on a ship" Minny paused for a moment before she finished her sentence. The thought of returning to Stone Shell made her extremely anxious.

"But we have no other option available to us."

Nectarion, who has been tentatively listening, closed his small book and approached the table. He studied the maps and reviewed the text from the books strewn across the table.

"This map, does anyone know what is beyond this point, over here, off the map?" he asked, pointing to the area west of the Fractured Anvil.

"As far as I am aware, the Syndicate has no information regarding what lies past that point; there is no ocean there, so no interest," Minny replied.

Nectarion moved to the journal and flicked through the pages of K.D.'s journey.

"Here, K.D. mentions something called the Anvil; perhaps he refers to this location here on the map."

"I noticed that too, but wasn't completely sure", Minny added.

"If we follow K.D.'s journey back through his journal, he mentions a forest north of where we found him, then further north, a ruin of an ancient city. Then there is his journey from east to west, originating in a place that could be this mountain." Nectarion followed a route that was off the map that could possibly reveal another way to reach the Fractured Anvil.

"That would mean that this northern region is not another continent but part of the same as Edron," said Siriana, an excitement in her voice at such a revelation.

"Well then, we have been presented with an alternative. It could take us some time to traverse this undiscovered territory, whereas travelling by ship will get us there relatively quickly." Announced Purvan.

"I would prefer, if we can, to avoid any serious dealings with the Syndicate", provided Minny.

"Is there a reason for that, something we should know about?" inquired Nectarion.

"It's not something I wish to discuss at this present moment," she explained, the party looking at her inquisitively."It's not an issue that should bother us as long as we don't have to associate with the Syndicate directly."

"I hope you're right, Minorha. You have been of great aid to us, so I believe I can speak for the whole group when I say, we will do our best to trust you," Purvan replied with a firm approach, ensuring Minny understood the position they were in.

"It's decided, we shall take the long way around."

On the morning of the next day, the party set out to organise their trip. Purvan and Siriana decided to approach the Lord Governor about a diplomatic pass that would allow them to travel through the realm under diplomatic immunity. He was able to grant this, presenting them with a parchment of Ambassadorial Appointment under the guise that they were looking to meet other people and open friendship and trade opportunities. He also stated that if the group acted outside these parameters and was apprehended, he would not be able to come to the party's aid and would have to deny all involvement for the safety of Edron. He finally said that when the party was ready to leave, they returned to the Keep.

After departing the Great Keep, Purvan turned to Siriana,

"Do you feel he knew something we don't?"

"How do you mean?"

"His posture and language usage suggest there is something more that our good friend Obo knows. I am a master of the tongue, and I can tell certain things when someone talks. I feel that there is more to this than he reveals."

The companions finished gathering their supplies and belongings and met in the market square, where it all began a few months ago. Purvan said his goodbyes to Siriana as she was to remain at the Hall of Mages and continue her work, which apparently had been lacking this past week. Purvan then led his friends back into the Great Keep, passing the guards who recognised the group and granted them entry. They ascended the stairs to the second level and found the Lord Governor there, sitting in his chair, behind his desk. As he noticed the party approach, he stood.

"Ah, good, you have returned. When Purvan explained what you plan to do, I felt that I could be of some assistance in getting you to your destination a little faster. This way, please."

He gestured for the party to move towards the wall nearby to the right. What looked like a solid wall that was a part of the structure was, in fact, a door that opened up into an antechamber. Entering the room, the companions saw that it was windowless. An individual appeared from a doorway on the far side of the room and stood near a pedestal with an orb atop. On the ground and occupying most of the floor space was a large circular platform with markings. There were twelve different runes placed at equal intervals between two circles that encompassed the outer edge of the raised stone platform. A line travelled from each rune to the centre, where a strange symbol lay.

"What is this?" Plutues asked, sensing an arcane energy about this room.

"This is a teleport circle or platform. It will transport you across great distances within an instant. It is one of five in all of Edron. The technology is relatively new and was actually discovered in the ruins that you have visited." Obo remarked.

"How come there are only five? This kind of magic could revolutionise travel," interjected Nectarion.

"Yes, well, as I said, it is relatively new, and the power requirements are exponential. Like all new things, it takes time. Perhaps in another fifty to a hundred years, there could be a teleport circle in every home." Lord Obo then gestured for the party to stand on the platform.

"So, how does it work? Will we be okay?" Oophaga asked as they cautiously stepped onto the circle.

"It has been tested and used many times, even by me and has yet to cause any side effects," the Lord Governor reassured them.

The party stood within the circle's perimeter, and the Lord Governor acknowledged the attendant standing near the orb. The Attendant placed their hand on the orb, and everyone noticed that an image appeared within. It looked like Westhold. Obo turned and took one last look at the party and said,

"Good luck."

A light encircled the outside of the platform, like a large arcane barrier between them and the Lord Governor. Four of the runes in the outer circle began to glow, and the arcane energy travelled from them to the centre, where the symbol there lit up. Then, each of the companions began to glow with arcane energy that sparkled blue, brighter and brighter. The forms of each changed into a ball of blue light that then shot upward. The arcane energy dissipated, the barrier faded, and the circle was empty.

A moment later, in the city of Westhold, the teleport circle lit up. The blue arcane barrier was active, and five blue balls of light descended from above and began to take form. Each of the party members reformed into their original selves and stood.

On the outside of the platform stood two individuals: an attendant next to an orb on a pedestal, and the other, a person of office.

There stood Lord Govenor Athalia Bazin, an Elvish female, reaching six and a half feet tall with long strawberry-blonde hair down to her knees. Her blonde hair had a pink tint running through it. She wore the attire of her office, but the red and puce colours of Westhold were not as dominant as her ruling counterparts, choosing to wear the colours under her white velvet chemise. It was kept to a minimum so as not to lose the colour of her hair. A chain draped between clasps that bore her badge of office as they held the mantle of her robes, her crown sat upon her strawberry blonde hair, and she wore several rings of silver and gold, some laid with gems upon her fingers.

124

"Welcome to Westhold. I have been awaiting your arrival. Lord Obo has apprised me of your quest, and I have prepared a means of travel for your party."

She then ushered the companions out of the chamber and led them to the Lord's Stable, where she presented the party with three horses.

"These should be of great use in your travels. I would also like to mention, I know of your relation to Stellda Furfoot and what you did in the Redwood Forest and wish to thank you, from all the people here in Westhold and all of Edron."

"You are welcome, my Lady," Purvan answered charmingly as he drew closer to her.

"Not now, Purvan!" Nectarion shouted.

With that, Purvan and his friends mounted their steeds and bid farewell to the Lord Governor.

The party travelled south back along the Silverleaf road and then turned onto the forest road they had traversed before. They made their way through the forest, passed Stellda's empty tower, and finally, after three days, reached the campsite where they had stayed before they had assaulted the Orc camp.

There was quiet on this night, but it was pleasant; the companions felt confident and excited. Random thoughts passed through some of their heads. Where was Nushala at this moment, and who was feeding Stellda's cats? The party showed Minny where they found the journal that belonged to someone with the initials K.D. and where he was buried.

The next day, the group continued to travel, now heading north, referring to the journal. Ooph with expectations of perhaps meeting some other druids that K.D. mentioned in his entries. As the sun began to set on the second day past the campsite, the party, now leading the horses on foot through the dense forest, had reached what they believed to be the loch mentioned in the journal. They decided to move north along the west bank and hopefully make contact with someone. As they slowly moved through the thickness of the trees, a noise could be heard, rustling. Just as they heard it, the party was ambushed, and six individuals, pointing sharp wooden spears at the party, stood there. Dressed in dark clothing, foliage and mud to blend into the forest like camouflage, there was no way the party would have noticed them even if they were standing right in front of them.

What started as six turned into twenty, as others hiding in the forest emerged. Three of the first six seized the horses from the party to prevent escape, while the other three pointed their weapons at the companions and took possession of their weapons.

"What should we do?" Minny asked.

"I suggest we don't make any sudden moves. I count over fifteen so far. Who knows how many more are lying in wait?" answered Ooph.

Without using any words, the forest folk motioned to the party to move in the direction they indicated.

"For now, let's just do what they want us to do."

Now completely surrounded by the forest folk, the party moved north in the direction they were being herded.

The trek through the forest was tedious and lengthy as the dense tree population restricted movement, and no clear path or trail was present. The horses made it even more complicated due to

126

their size. After travelling for the better part of the day, the forest folk had finally led the group into a clearing. The sun had set a few hours ago, and the starry night sky had taken hold. After the forest canopy had blocked the sky all day, it was pleasant to see openness.

Before them was a small village that rested on the west side of the Loch, which can now be clearly seen by the lack of trees in the camp. The moonlight shone across its still surface. The village consisted of hut-like structures made from logs, with branches and foliage on the rooftops. A small gathering area, circled with logs and centred with a campfire blazing, was situated between the huts and the loch. Each of the huts had a totem placed out the front, each depicting various adornments such as fur, feathers, claws and even the bones of some animals. As the party surveyed the rest of the village, they found it comprised mostly of Elves and Humans, but there was at least one Infernis, a Dwarf, a Drakona and a few Ribbet.

The party was escorted to a log around the campfire and motioned to sit. The horses were led away, and the party's weapons were taken by one of the individuals who went over to a hut very near the circle. A few moments passed, and the individual returned with someone.

Approaching the party was a female elf with long dark hair and olive tanned skin. Wearing animal skins and simple leather and cloth, browns and greens. On her head, she wore a crown of flowers intertwined with vines and leaves. She, like the rest of the inhabitants here, was barefoot.

"My people have been tracking you since you entered our territory." The Elf said abruptly as she sat on the log opposite the party. "What is your purpose here?"

Pluteus spoke first, "We are peaceful travellers and we are just passing through."

"Travellers, you say, we don't get many outsiders coming through here. As a matter of fact, we don't get anyone passing through here."

"We were unaware that this forest was off limits, we didn't mean to trespass, and we are not hostile to you or your people. Let me introduce myself and my companions. I am Nectarion Seraphix. This is Purvan, Pluteus, Oophaga and Minorha," he gestured to his friends as he announced their names.

The Elvish woman looked at the party, sizing them up and determining whether to trust them or not. She paid particular attention to Ooph, a druid.

"My name is Reyah, and this is my tribe or circle, if you will."

"Circle, what do you mean by that?" inquired Purvan.

"A circle is what you call a group or clan of druid folk," explained Reyah.

At this, Ooph's attention was piqued.

"So you are all druids that live here?" they asked.

"Not all, some of us are trackers, rangers."

"Are you their leader?" queried Nectarion.

"Not so much. I am more of a facilitator. I help maintain order and peace. No one is forced to be here, and no one is ordered to do anything, but there is an understanding. If you are part of this village, you contribute in some way. Like nature, we are all connected."

The party listened to Reyah attentively, waiting for the druid's intent regarding their presence within their forest. While her gaze was locked on Ooph, she continued.

"We will allow you to stay the night in our village, but I ask you to move on in the morning. My people will escort you to the forest's edge in whatever direction you wish."

The party's body language showed relief as they now realised that the druids weren't going to become hostile toward them. Reyah gestured to her fellow villagers to come over and show the party where they could rest for the night. After settling in, the group mingled with the villagers and learned about them. They discovered an old tribal story about an adventurer who passed through the forest several hundred seasons ago and ascertained that it was the owner of the journal. Nectarion gave the village a supply of his nectar and showed them how to store it. Minny decided to take the opportunity to have a dip in the loch, diving and skimming along the bottom of the loch between the water life.

Finally, the companions retired to the beds, and amongst the sounds of the forest, the nightlife filled their ears; they managed to find sleep.

Chapter Nine

The party lay still in their beds, deep in sleep. The icy chill of the morning rested on their uncovered faces. The silence was broken by a quiet thud, but the party did not stir. Another soft thud, this time Purvan was startled and cracked an eye to see what the source was. As he sat up, a third thud hit him in the chest. The source of the noise was a small rock, a pebble. Another entered the hut, this time hitting Pluteus. Purvan placed his hand on his companion and jolted him to wake up as another pebble flew into the hut, hitting Oophaga this time. They sat up instantly after being hit in the back of the head.

A voice could now be heard from outside, speaking in an unknown language.

"What are they saying?"

"It's Druidic, they are telling us to wake up. I am a little out of practice, but I am pretty sure he called us tenderfoots," Oophaga translated.

"Tenderfoots, what is that meant to imply?"

"They think we are soft, not used to being out here in the wild. Although there is something lost in the translation, it's much more of an insult than that."

After a short time, the party exited the hut, awake and ready. The sky was still dark with a slight glow of light in the east. A small group of druids and rangers stood ready near the cold fireplace. One individual, a male Drakonan, approached the group.

"My name is Maroc. I will be leading the hunting party this morning."

"Pleasure to meet you, Maroc." Purvan extended his hand to shake.

Maroc simply looked down at the Halfling, making no move to reciprocate.

"Just do what I tell you and stay close to the group, don't wander and don't make any noise". And he walked back to his fellow villagers.

The hunting party had been travelling for over an hour, making their way south close to the edge of the loch. They had been following the tracks of a few boars and were very close. Each of the companions was spread out and accompanied by one of the villagers to babysit them. Minorha and her partner were very close to the bank of the loch. Her ranger partner stopped a moment for a drink when Minny noticed something in the water. She moved closer to inspect the situation and found dead fish floating on the surface of the water.

The ranger noticed this as well and looked at Minny with concern. The ranger made a small noise, like an animal call of some sort, and after a moment, another ranger and a druid appeared. One of the rangers picked up a dead fish, held it to their nose and took a whiff. In disgust, they threw it back.

"It is not of natural causes," he exclaimed.

The druid, now crouching down close to the water's edge, waved their hand over the lifeless fish bodies, and a slight glow of magic energy emanated from their fingers.

"There is definitely a poison here, not natural, a corruption plagues these creatures, and the loch. We must return at once and inform Reyah."

By now, the rest of the hunting party had discovered the scene, two carrying their quarry from the hunt. The others explained the situation, and the hunting party gathered itself and began its return to the village with haste.

Reyah, Maroc, the party and a few others stood just outside Reyah's hut, discussing what they had discovered. Nearby, the campfire was roaring with flame as the two boars were roasting, and the village was busy preparing to break fast.

"Once we have had our meal, you, Maroc and three others will accompany me to the Sacred Grove. Redhusk will be able to guide us in this matter."

"Who is Redhusk?" Minny queried.

"It's not important for you to know, your time here is almost done. Our people will escort you to the edge of the forest as agreed," Maroc firmly stated.

"Maroc's right, we thank you for your assistance, but this is a matter for us, we are the protectors of the forest."

Oophaga stepped forward, "Reyah, please let us help. Let me help. I am a child of nature as much as the rest of you. I can feel the pain of this corruption and wish to do what I can."

Reyah looked into Ooph's large black eyes and could see, could feel the sorrow, just like what she herself felt. A moment of complete silence passed, and looking at Ooph and their friends, Reyah finally spoke.

"I sense a great potential in you, Oophaga. We may need your skill in due time. I will allow you to accompany us."

With the fast broken, the village began to engage in its daily chores. Reyah and her fellow villagers joined with the party and set out, leaving the village behind. Along the way, Reyah and the others told the tale of Redhusk, an ancient oak tree that held mystical powers of nature and would guide the druids in times of need. Centuries old, the tree is said to have a connection, or did, to the goddess of nature, the Nurturing Mother, Yna.

The expedition had spent the better part of the day travelling south along the edge of the Marr Loch. They had stopped for the midday meal and were on their way again. The party noticed more dead fish in the loch, and some of the plant life had started to show signs of withering. They also discovered a dark green, viscous ooze that had formed on the plant life. The druids examined it and ascertained that it was connected to the problem they were attending to. As the group drew closer to the Sacred Tree, they began to notice more dead animals that had rotted mostly away, giving off an unnatural smell of decay.

Reyah examined the bodies of the decaying animals, while Maroc stood close by. Ooph could tell he was communicating with the plant life, his hand upon the trunk of a nearby tree.

"These poor beasts have been affected," Reyah stated.

Maroc turned to her, "Yes, the forest informs me that these creatures have not passed even a day."

Looking at the corpses, the decay indicated that it had been a few weeks.

"What could do something like this? There is more than corruption here; there is darkness. Evil."

The druids all took a moment as they seemed to be suffering from some kind of pain or nausea. Maroc handed everyone a small berry.

"Here, this should help somewhat. Come, we must keep moving. The day is almost over, and it is not far to the Sacred Tree of Marr."

As the sun began its final stretch, dropping behind the tree tops in the west of the forest, the expedition reached the Sacred Grove of Redhusk. The grove was somewhat open, and the trees were spaced away from each other. Other plants, such as ferns and palms, filled the spaces between. The ground was covered in leaves that had fallen and vines that travelled from here to there. On the other side of the grove stood a massive tree that must have been four hundred feet tall, with a wide girth, much larger than any of the other trees seen in the forest. The same viscous ooze could be seen on all the plant life throughout the grove, and the Sacred Tree itself showed green glowing veins ascending its trunk.

"This is not how this should look; the corruption here is intense and more powerful than anywhere else." The looks on Reyah and her fellow druids' faces showed their heartbreak.

A noise from the trees could be heard, and there was movement. The forest came alive, and emerging from the trees, two individuals moved towards the group. They appeared to be feminine, but they had green skin, and what looked like clothing was actually vines, foliage and tree bark covering their bodies.

Their hair was filled with twigs and vines and almost looked like a bird's nest.

The party were startled and began to ready themselves to deal with a threat.

"It's okay, they won't harm you, they are the Grove Guardians." Maroc quickly explained.

Reyah approached the guardians

"What happened here? What is this corruption?"

In a feminine voice that echoed through the grove, one of the guardians answered.

"The Sacred Tree is ill and dying. Corruption, darkness. We tried to keep it contained, but it has finally spread to the other parts of the forest"

"I don't understand what they are saying," Purvan responded, confused.

"It is druidic, they say the tree is dying." Ooph translated, sadness in their voice.

Reyah and her fellow druids approached the party and explained the full situation.

"These Dryads have explained the situation. If something isn't done soon, we will lose the Sacred Tree. But there may be a way to reverse the corruption, expel it from Redhusk and return the forest to its natural state. An old druidic ritual"

"I have heard of such a ritual, but I have never seen it performed," expressed Ooph.

"It will require all of us to circle the tree and concentrate our energy into it, and hopefully push the corruption out. It shouldn't be difficult, but it is a strain on the body and will drain you, leaving you exhausted afterwards."

"We must try, Reyah. It is too important, we can not let the Sacred Tree die, it will affect not just this forest but the balance of nature overall." Maroc pleaded.

Reyah nodded in agreement and gestured that the druids, including Oophaga, circle the tree.

"This is old magic; there is no incantation. It simply requires us to connect with one another through the bonds of nature with a single thought, one goal, to heal Redhusk."

Standing with their arms extended out around the tree, they closed their eyes and began to concentrate. Within their palms, the energy of nature was brought forth and formed. The light from the magic glowed and lit up the grove in the dark of the evening. The tree itself began to glow as well, the druid's magic working its will. The tree trunk opened up, and within the centre of it, a large object emanated a green energy.

Looking closely at the ritual and the tree, the rest of the party could see the object inside the tree. Their faces donned looks of surprise as they recognised the shape and size of the object. A crystal that looked about a foot tall and sat on a round base, almost exactly the same as the one they delivered to Stellda, the only difference is that this one is green.

Behind the party, the two dryads stand poised, but there was a sudden shift in their stance. They began to convulse, the bark on the bodies splintered and formed sharp barbs, the vines tightened, and as they looked up again at the scene, their eyes glowed an eerie yellow.

Startled by the movement from behind, Pluteus and Minny turned to face the Grove Guardians. On the other side of the grove, Purvan and Nectarion noticed two more appear from the trees. Not

136

sure how to respond, the party remained vigilant. The first reached Pluteus and went to attack, but he blocked it with his staff and moved back. Purvan and Nectraion moved towards the other two as they drew close to the druids, noticing their intent.

Vines that grew out from Redhusk began to come alive and moved like tentacles. They moved towards Nectarion and Purvan. Nectarion flew up, but Purvan was wrapped up in vines and held to a nearby tree, unable to move. From behind Reyah, the trees came alive. These were not like the dryads, but actual trees that began to move, and they started to make their way towards the druids in their ritual. Maroc could see them behind Reyah.

"*Help!* Treants. They are trying to prevent us from performing the ritual. Do something, mushroom head."

With this, Pluteus summoned an Ice Spike and drove it toward the small group of living trees, hitting its mark. It pierced the centre treant, and it shattered, sending small ice needles projecting out and severely damaging the other treants nearby.

"*Maintain your concentration; if we falter, that ritual will fail and the tree will be lost!*" shouting out, Reyah encouraged the others to continue.

Close by to Pluteus, Minny swung her bulking mace made of a hunk of wood and hit one of the Dryads coming towards her, sending it back, and it almost toppled over. Pluteus was engaged with the other close by, using his staff as a weapon, like a quarterstaff, until the Dryad finally succumbed to its injuries and fell to the ground. Just as the party felt they were making headway, two more Dryads appeared from the forest, and the first summoned a cage of vines and wood, trapping Pluteus.

Minny continued to swing her weapon, becoming an unstoppable force and striking down another Dryad. On the other side of the tree behind Reyah, more treants appeared. Nectarion, having dispatched two of the dryads, flew over the tree tops and behind the treants. He landed right behind them and swung his Hallowed axe, and with one swoop of his weapon, the treants were cleaved in half.

"Timber, *motherfuckers*."

The druids, who were now reaching the end of the ritual, showed signs of extreme exhaustion and tried all they could to hold on just a little bit longer. Minny finished off her current opponent as it dropped to the ground. Pluteus busted out of his confinement and fired another Ice Spike at another Dryad, sending it down, and Nectarion rejoined them as they regrouped for the next wave. A moment passed, and the Grove Guardians had ceased to come forth. The party looked at Redhusk and noticed the intense power the druids had created.

In the centre of the grove, an orb of negative arcane energy began to form, cancelling out any sound around the grove and deafening the group momentarily. An entity of chaotic magic formed - a Chaos Elemental. Swirls of dark purple and magenta mixed with black smoke appeared as a bipedal creature that now towered before the party.

"*What the hell is it?!*" yelled Minny, alarmed.

"*Very bad is what?!*" shouted Pluteus, detecting the chaotic energy.

A shockwave of magic ploughed over the grove, ripping leaves and branches from their growth. The party was thrown and landed on the grove's edge, lying in the crushed foliage. The Chaos Elemental moved to attack the druids, just as a final burst of druidic magic cleansed the tree, and a green shockwave expanded out across the grove, dissipating the Chaos Elemental before it could continue its rampage. The Sacred Tree regained its vibrant look, and the ooze that covered the plant life no longer existed as it dissolved quickly into nothing.

The druids all dropped to the ground, out of breath and completely drained. The party made their way over and tended to them, making sure they were not in any danger of dying.

"Hey, do you think someone could let me out now?" Purvan yelled from the tree he is tied to. Minny went over and loosened the vines, releasing Purvan.

Reyah got to her feet, Nectarion holding her up. She moved toward Redhusk and placed her hand on its trunk.

"Are you okay now, old friend?"

"*I live because of you. Thank you for your kindness.*"

"What happened? What was the corruption that affected you?"

"*It was a great evil, a darkness is coming, and it had begun to take root here in my grove.*"

"What is this evil you speak of?"

"*An evil older than I, of primordial nature.*"

"Where is this evil? Where does it come from?"

"*The source is unknown, but there is an evil rising in the south. It has the same aura as that which almost consumed me.*"

"Thank you, my friend, rest now and recover your strength."

Now that night had fallen and everyone was tired, the group decided to rest for the night in the grove. The guardians had reappeared, broken from their violent nature. They assured the group that the grove was in full recovery and that they would help nurture Redhusk back to full health. Despite their victory, there was still a feeling of melancholy through the party. This talk of a darkness that was apparently still out there made the win somewhat hollow. To break the silence around the campfire, Pluteus asked a question.

"What was that energy in the centre of the tree, the green glowy thing?"

The druids all looked at each other, and then Reyah answered.

"That is the Heart of the Tree. It is what gives Redhusk its life and intelligence."

"Is it the only one? Do other trees have one?"

"No, it is the only one we know of."

The party all turned to look at each other, knowing that they had already seen one. The group fell silent again, and one by one, each curled up in their beds and fell asleep, Ooph being the last. Before they lay down to rest, they approached Redhusk and placed their frog hand on the tree.

"Ancient tree, do you know much about the object inside you, your *heart*, as it is called?"

"I know that it is an ancient and powerful magical item, set within me long ago by druids to create a strong conduit between them and the goddess, Yna."

"Are there any more in existence?"

A momentary pause occurs before Redhusk responds.

"There is, there are others, but I am unaware of their location or their purpose."

Oophaga stood there for a moment before they retracted their hand and returned to their bedroll. The night crawled on slowly, and it was some time before Ooph found actual sleep.

The journey back to the village the next day was relatively quiet, and yet the group did feel a sense of accomplishment after cleansing Redhusk. They entered the village just after the sun had set, and the villagers were glad to see them. They informed Reyah that the evening before was eventful, as the whole village felt the forest at its moment of need and the sudden relief afterwards. Reyah, Maroc and the others, in turn, retold the tale of the ritual and saving the Sacred Tree.

The companions were granted one more night in the village before they would leave in the morning, and as they sat around the evening fire, Reyah beckoned Oophaga to join her in her hut.

"I have to tell you something, Ooph. Firstly, you performed well in the grove; you have an exceptional power. Where do you come from, what circle?"

Reluctant at first, Ooph looked at Reyah and sensed trust.

"I originated from a grove in the east, along the north coast. We never had a name for our village, no mention of a circle."

"The east, you say. I don't retain much knowledge of the outside world, just what has been passed down. It has been said that this village, this circle, originated from the east. It may be possible that my people are descendants of yours."

Ooph looked at Reyah attentively at this revelation as she continued.

"If this is the case, then you could be from what we refer to as the First Circle. Ooph, it is important that you know something else, something Redhusk told me. Druids are going to play an important role in the future. A darkness is coming, an evil, and we are to play a key part in the greater conflict. You may be called upon for something more. Something to think about on your travels"

Oophaga remained silent, letting the information sink in, processing it all. Reyah handed Ooph a mug of tea.

"Don't let it consume you, my friend, but keep it close to the surface of your mind. I can sense in you something special, and you may discover something on your journey."

Chapter Ten

The party rose on the morning after. They had a small meal, collected their gear, their horses and farewelled the villagers. Reyah wished them luck and gave particular attention to Ooph as she said it. Maroc, the Drakonan, and two others escorted the companions to the western edge of the forest.

"If you head south, that way, you should eventually find yourself in Tarin Marr. If you continue north as you had intended, you will ultimately find the villages in the grasslands."

Maroc paused a moment, as if to collect himself. "It was agreeable to have met you all, and on behalf of our people, we thank you. Please be safe in your travels."

"Thank you, Maroc. Hopefully, we'll see you again," Purvan said graciously.

"Hopefully not," he replied gruffly, and with that, Maroc and his two associates turned and headed back the way they came.

The party watched as they disappeared into the trees and then turned their attention to their own.

"Well, my friends, which way should we make?" Nectarion put forward.

"I think we should continue north and find this library we seek", Pluteus eagerly injected.

"What about this 'so-called' evil in the south. Should we investigate that? Purvan asked inquisitively.

"I don't believe now is the right time. I believe seeking knowledge will be the key," continued Pluteus.

143

The party all nodded in agreement, mounted their steeds and began their trek north.

Using the adventurer's journal and the compass that didn't point true north, the party ascertained that the compass could actually be the adventurer's. It was very old, and looking at the maps, it was pointing in the direction of the Fractured Anvil. The group traversed the edge of the Forest of Marr for a couple of days until they reached a river that fed into the forest. This was most likely the one K. D. mentioned in the journal. The party followed the river north, loosely guided by the compass's direction and into the grassy plains of the Kishar Grasslands.

They travelled easterly across the grasslands for the next few days without incident, a pleasant change from recent events. The grasslands were wide open with slight inclinations from time to time. Trees were sparsely seen, cropping up in groups of four or five, or sometimes just one on its own. The trees were large oak types and provided a great source of shade, and the party had been lucky to utilise them for camp.

During the sixth day since their departure from the forest, the party happened across a dirt road, travelling in a west-to-east direction. Signs of wheel tracks within the dirt indicated civilisation, although the group believed it had been some time since anyone had passed.

"It seems we are on the right track," jested Purvan. "Did you see what I did there?" he said with a humorous grin on his face.

"Shall we continue east along this road?" Minorha queried.

"I think we continue east. This road must lead somewhere, and the druids did mention villages," suggested Pluteus enthusiastically.

And without hesitation, the party started following the road east.

Rain began to fall heavily on the party as they trekked through the wet weather. Minny enjoyed the calming scent of the rain, and Ooph rejoiced in the moisture refreshing their skin. Pluteus' robes flowed with fresh growth as the damp conditions were perfect for him. Nectarion was very vocal about his wings being wet, and Purvan bemoaned the ruin of his second favourite pair of soft leather boots. For the past few days, the weather had been dismal to some, and the party had found it difficult to stay protected, save for the few trees out on the grasslands that had provided some shelter from the rain.

The clouds finally rolled over, the rain ceased to fall, and a clear sky became visible. Here and there, the party passed farmlands and could see small homesteads that rested off in the distance. While still grey and cloudy, the party found themselves approaching what looked like a town. Could this be one of the villages they were informed about? The party, mounted on their horses, with Pluteus walking alongside and Nectarion hovering just above, entered the village on the wet and muddy road that intersected the village centre.

Rustic-style log buildings lined the sides of the thoroughfare, but these structures are not like those of the small towns in Edron. The woodwork was not rough-hewn but refined and worked. Straight edges and smooth, rounded curves, the clay

145

tiles of the roofs were perfectly placed and even. The windows on shop fronts have brill glass panes and the finishings were flawless. While the buildings do not show any magnificent designs or filigree, the simple work still came across as exemplary.

The buildings were also spaced out somewhat and not cramped close together. Most of them rested on small stumps to lift them off the ground to allow for level floorwork. While there was no signage on the buildings, the purpose and use of each building was quite obvious. A store that would be a supplier of general goods and equipment, another with clothing displayed must be a tailor. A barn-like building with two large open doors, which was obviously a livery and blacksmith, had an individual who could be seen working on an anvil, with a horse fastened nearby. Some of the structures looked like large storehouses. The sound of machinery from within, grinding noises, reminded the party of a mill. At the far end of the thoroughfare, a small building with a steeple and two sizable wooden doors that had a very pious motif about it. And of course, no town is complete without a tavern.

Trotting through the soft, wet dirt of the main road, the party slowly made their way further into the centre of this town. After noticing the craftsmanship of the buildings, the next thing they noticed was the people, going about their business, but also all eyes were on the party as they came into closer proximity. They noticed that they were all Elves, and for rural folk, they were well-dressed in quality attire. Whispers could be heard but not understood, except by Purvan.

"It's Elvish, of course," he explained quietly to his friends.

A man loading a wagon next to a produce shop looked and accidentally dropped the crate he was carrying; the round green foodstuff was now sinking into the mud.

"Bloody hell, my cabbages." Purvan could hear him say.

The party finally reached the tavern, hitching rails out front, and a couple of horses were already tied up to them. The party had eyes still locked on them from the townsfolk, a sense of curiosity from the denizens, as if they had never seen anything like them before.

The tavern, in keeping with the rest of the town, was just as beautifully built. Not a piece out of place, not a knot or a hole in any of the woodwork. The party stepped up onto the front veranda that stretched about fifty feet along the front side of the building. Four large glass windows occupied the face of the tavern. One window, the main door and then another three before the end. At the other end, enough space for a fifth window was instead taken up by a large noticeboard. Purvan approached the board to find anything interesting.

"Apparently, Zoas is looking for someone with a prime bull to mate with his cow."

His companions looked at him, unfazed by this tidbit of information.

"Let's see if the welcome in here is as warm as what we have already encountered", stated Nectarion.

"Don't worry, if they try something, I'll be ready". Minny declared quietly.

As the companions entered the tavern, an air of silence fell over the entire establishment, as again, all eyes were on the party. Just as the outside was, the inside was just as marvellous. There

147

was minimal decoration, but the fine craftsmanship was present. Three more windows were in the far wall, looking out onto the grasslands behind the tavern. The bar itself was the most ˙ extraordinary piece. Despite its simplistic design, it was a perfect example of carpentry. A moment passed, and the party decided to move towards the bar.

In the common tongue, Nectarion opened a dialogue,

"Greetings, friend. My companions and I have been travelling all week, and in the rain, we are looking for a good warm meal and drink."

The Elvish male barkeep turned to the party, his work apron dirty yet somehow still quite presentable as opposed to other barkeepers. He looked the party up and down and answered in a welcoming tone.

"Sure, comrade, our lunch menu is open, we have beef, pork and chicken with a side of greens and a mug of ale." The Elf's voice was slightly rustic yet very pleasant and not coarse.

The party ordered their desired food and placed a few gold coins on the counter. Pluteus opted for an all-green meal.

"Take a seat, I'll bring it out when it's done"

The barkeep headed into the kitchen via a door behind the bar, and the party found a table in the far corner, sat and waited.

"It is an interesting place, very lovely despite the constant stares. Do you think they have a fascination with everyone they come across?"

Pluteus looked at Nectarion and answered, "Maybe we're just the new kids on the block."

After a short while, the barkeep brought out the party's meals and drinks, smiled at them and returned to his station. Being the midday meal, patrons of the tavern came and went, and it was quite busy, despite being a small town in the middle of nowhere. The party enjoyed the meal and tentatively watched the townsfolk come and go while maintaining their stares.

Remaining seated for a short while afterwards, Nectarion finally returned to the barkeep.

"Excuse me, good sir, we are explorers passing through this region and wondered if we could learn more about you and your town, your people."

"What would you like to know?"

"History, culture, that sort of thing."

"Well, I don't see an issue with that, but I'm not the person you should ask."

"Who should I ask then?"

"The town Seraph. They keep the records of our town. If you're looking for something, you'll most likely find it there. The building on the right at the end of the road with the pointed roof."

Nectarine acknowledged the barkeep's assistance and signalled his friends to leave. They exited the tavern and walked towards the end of the street to the small, pious-looking building. The door on the left was open, and the group entered. The outside, while beautifully crafted, did not show the internal elegance. Of all the buildings, this would have to be the most artistic. While remaining in conformity with the rest of the village, there were noticeable designs that jumped out at the group. Pews lined each side of the small building, and glass windows that looked out occupied the walls on either side. The pews, wooden bench seats, had elegant filigree on the arms, smooth and rounded as opposed to their straight, rigid, square design.

At the far end, a dias stood central to the aisle that bisected the pews. A gradine lined the wall behind the dias with several small candles placed upon it. A female Elf was currently lighting candles when she noticed the party enter. She had long blonde hair and was wearing simple and yet fine quality clothing similar to that of a clergy person; A long white robe with a blue ephod and sash, and a white translucent veil upon her head.

"Welcome to our small shrine, may prayer be with you." She announced, looking very curious at the entourage of unusual individuals.

Pluteus stepped forward nervously,

"Good day, sir. Would you be able to give us some guidance?"

"Pluteus, that's a woman," Purvan says, correcting him while giving her a sultry stare; his gaze showed his visual appreciation.

"My apologies, pinkskins all look the same to me."

She looked at the party with bemusement and continued

"What guidance do you seek, friend? I can give you spiritual guidance; it is what I am here for."

"Oh no, we are looking for knowledge, information. The history of your town and people, any records that may help us on our journey."

"I find it fascinating why outsiders would be interested in our humble town's history, but I have no qualms in allowing you to peruse our records. Please wait here until I return."

With that, she entered a door that led to a back room and returned about ten minutes later with her arms full of scrolls, parchment and a few tomes.

"If you need any assistance, please ask. I would be happy to help."

The party spent the next few hours reading through the various documents. Births, weddings and deaths of the townsfolk. The Seraphs of the town also documented when strangers came to town. Small footnotes, really nothing that you would write home about. After looking back far enough, there was a mention of an individual with a pet fox who passed through the town approximately seven hundred years ago before leaving to head south, exploring.

During the party's research, Purvan and the Seraph slipped away discreetly, and after a few moments, the rest of the party began to hear strange noises from a short distance away. What started as a series of whimpers and murmurs escalated to moans of ecstasy, and what must have been the Seraph's sweet voice, culminated in a high-pitched squeal of absolute pleasure. Some moments passed, and both the Seraph and Purvan returned to the main hall. Purvan's appearance looked as if he hadn't even broken a sweat, his hair still perfectly quaffed, but the Seraph had dishevelled hair, and her garments were not readjusted to their original perfect state.

The history of the town was intertwined with four other towns in the Kishar Grasslands. Thousands of years ago, a great city, the city of Kishar, was the pinnacle of Elvish civilisation. Art, philosophy, religion, magic and science were all well advanced beyond most other cultures. Then it fell to ruin; the tomes don't indicate how, just that it fell to ruin. The surviving citizens migrated south, all their culture and technology lost. They eventually founded small settlements and led simple lives.

151

One tome that the group found interesting and all had a read of was a compilation of legends and fairy tales from the region.

****

The Great Battle - *During the height of the city's existence, there was a great siege of the city by 80 Ogres from the forests in the north. For 217 days, the ogres surrounded the city and prevented the inhabitants from leaving. Neighbouring villages and cities could not get to the City of Kishar, and all trade had come to a standstill until Lord Bardon, brother to the King's Wife of Kishar, mounted a force with another kingdom in the east to march on the ogres and free the city.*

The Apostle - *The City of Kishar is where the Apostle originated from. The Apostle was a single individual who travelled the lands and spread the word of the gods, to live in harmony and peace.*

The Fire Storm - *One time, the city came under threat from a storm of fire and brimstone. For three days, it rained fire from the sky, during which the great wizard Moonshadow created a magical barrier that protected the city. He stood in the centre of the city for those three days with no rest, food or water until he knew the city was safe.*

The Girl and the Hare - *There is a story about a girl, a simple farmer's daughter, who apparently chased a hare and fell down a hole. Her father rounded up his three farmhands (Straws, Tinnie* *and Leo) and they tried for hours into the night to retrieve her from the hole, only to discover her lying in a ditch the next morning, not far from where she fell. The most interesting part is the girl's recollection of her time in the hole, talking cats and smoking caterpillars and a green wizard that tried to chop off her head.*

****

By the end of the day, the party had had their fill of research, and while they had found the information fascinating, they really had not made any progress. No new information was gained, but the companions still felt they were on the right track.

"What do we do now? The sun is setting. Perhaps we should stay the night and head out in the morning." Oophaga suggested.

Overhearing, the Seraph, whom Purvan had shared, was named Selphie, spoke out.

"You are more than welcome. The clerk at the General Store, Darshee, she has a back room that you could utilise."

The party all agreed and thanked Selphie for her time and assistance. The companions headed to the store and asked the clerk for permission to use the back room for the night, which she readily agreed to. They then headed back to the tavern for the evening meal. By now, most of the townsfolk had come into town for their usual evening revelry. Even farmers who lived outside of the town centre had attended.

This was obviously the norm for the town; they worked hard and would all come into town for relaxation and social interaction. The party and townsfolk had become much more

153

relaxed now, warming up to each other. They drank and talked, shared their stories, tales and history. The barkeep, Corym, even gave out free drinks for an hour or so, which made everyone happy.

The end of the night came, and the townsfolk eventually made their way home. The party retired to the back room of the General Store, which once served as the clerk's small apartment until they moved out. It is the first night in a week that companions had a decent rest, and it took only moments for them to drift into sleep.

The next morning, the party packed up their horses, said their goodbyes to the townsfolk, and headed east out of town towards their destination. Travelling across the grasslands, the wet weather long behind them, they felt a sense of accomplishment in finding some new friends.

The grasslands had started to come to an end as the tree population began to grow and close the gaps between them. The townsfolk of Afen, as they had discovered was its name, had mentioned that the party would soon meet the edge of a forest in the east. The companions assumed that this was probably the one mentioned in the journal, and the compass was pointing in that direction. Upon reading the journal again, Pluteus discovered that the adventurer never mentioned the villages in the Kishar Grasslands and found it incredibly curious as to why. He also noticed that the pages missing were in between his discovery of the ruins and his meeting with the Druids of Marr, right where he could have written about the villages.

During the next few days of travel, the group went without incident. However, Nectarion had a peculiar sense of dread that he could not shake off. Since the village, he had been catching glimpses of a large, black, mangy dog. He first noticed it back in the village and thought nothing of it; perhaps it belonged to one of the townsfolk. But for it to still be present was unusual, and its ability to appear and then disappear was uncanny.

After three days, Nectarion mentioned the sightings to the rest of his friends.

"I have seen that dog too," Minny added. "Big, black and scraggly?"

"Yes, the same. This is extremely unsettling"

"What do you think we should do?" Oophaga asked.

"And what do you think it means?" Minny added.

"Well, I know of a myth or superstition about a large black dog representing an omen of death. There have been many sightings over hundreds of years, but no substantial evidence that this creature actually exists." Nectarion recalled. "It could be this animal, the description certainly matches, and it is often referred to as the Grimm."

"Yes, I am familiar with the tale as well." Purvan added, "There are a few songs of the Grimm written in many bardic tomes."

"Should we confront this creature, draw it out?" Minny suggested feistily. "Perhaps we should backtrack, try and find this dog."

"I don't think we should get ahead of ourselves; it could just be a stray dog." Pluteus speculated.

"I would agree, except for the shadow that has been growing in my mind these past days, I would have mentioned it before, except I wanted to be sure," resolved Nectarion. "We have to be careful, if this truly is the Grimm, it could mean one or even all of us is about to meet our end."

The party decided that if they were going to die, they should meet their death head-on and return along the route they had been travelling. At the turn of the next day, as they were casually but cautiously keeping an eye out, they were startled suddenly by the very creature they were seeking.

Before them was a large black scraggly dog with matted hair. It approached the party ever so slightly. This animal, if you could call it that, was the size of a small horse. The group could feel it sizing them up. Its lips curled up, saliva dripping, yellow eyes so vibrant, you would think they are glowing. A slight growl came forward from the beast as it lifted its nose to the air, smelling their scent, their fear. The party readied itself for an attack.

"Careful, we don't know its actual intentions". Nectarion stated.

Nectarion moved forward slightly, and Minny followed close behind while the rest of the party remained still. As they drew closer, it stood up on its hind legs, its muscle composition changing, bones cracked and shifted, the creature's hair instantly becoming clean and straight, gorgeous, soft fur of black and grey. A black, tattered, hooded robe covered its head and flowed behind it in the wind. Its snout was just visible outside the hood, but they could still see its eyes, those deep, vibrant yellow eyes that could penetrate an individual's soul.

"Stand down," Minny commanded firmly. Nectarion's usual gentle hum of his wings grew louder as their speed increased.

"Someone should go talk to it?" suggested Purvan.

Nectarion and Minorha looked at each other and cautiously continued to move forward, ever so slightly. As they did, the creature retrieved a weapon from seemingly nowhere inside his cloak. A long black shaft with curved blades on each end, runes engraved around the edges of the sickle-like blades, glowing in a dark purplish colour of magical aura. It held the weapon by its side, a show of power and strength.

Minorha and Nectarion halted, standing about ten metres now from the towering creature.

"You are Minorha, I can see into your soul, I know your fear and your desires. You fear failure and desire a better world to live in. You are Nectarion, you fear the fall of your people, and you desire vengeance."

"How do you know so much about us? Who are you? What is your purpose here?" Nectarion demanded.

"My purpose is to ferry souls across the veil. I am Death."

"Why does Death follow us?"

"Death will come for you eventually, but you all have a destiny. What follows you is the death of others."

"Are you saying that the village we just visited is dead?" Minny asked anxiously.

"They are at risk, just as we all are; there is a darkness coming."

"Why does death follow us?" Minny continued.

"There are those that destiny calls upon in times of need, based on what is in the heart and soul.

"Do you mean we are chosen?" Nectarion questioned.

"You have potential, we all have potential, but can you live up to those expectations?"

"Do you have a path for us to follow? Can you tell us where to go?"

"I can not tell you where to go; you must decide. I am here to simply guide you."

"Who sent you?" asked Minny.

"My mother."

"Who is your mother?"

"You do not know her, but she knows you. She is your mother, too."

Nectarion and Minny turned to their companions, who had been close behind listening, and there was a confounded look on everyone's face.

"So you can't help us in any way?

"I will say only this: your destination will yield reward, but the more time you take, the more the darkness will take hold. Do not wait too long to act."

The party gathered together and talked amongst themselves.

"Are we really going to listen to this creature? We only just met, and it wants us to trust it," expressed Pluteus.

"There is definitely a divine energy that I can sense, something very powerful. It could be one of the old gods." Ooph explained.

"I am just saying, until we know for sure that this creature is not full of shit, we should just be cautious."

"No faith, my friend." Nectarion directed at Pluteus. "Can you not sense its magic aura?"

"Yes, but that could be anything, something else posing as a divine entity. I can feel it isn't lying, but he could be an agent of evil trying to steer us wrong. There is something it is not telling us."

The discussion between Pluteus and Nectarion began to escalate as the other watched and listened to the two discuss the philosophies of faith and logic.

"I think it's important we listen to this creature; it obviously has power enough to know things about us."

"You can't just commit to something without some form of assurance; it's not very rational. This whole thing could be a scam. Do you seriously believe in everything?"

"Well, before I met you, I was completely unaware of your people. Now I discover there are talking mushrooms in the world."

Discontent with waiting for the party to respond, the creature known as Death interrupted.

"I must now depart; the way lies with you, choose."

He sniffed the air and continued.

"I am being called. I wish you well."

Pluteus noticed that the direction he looked as he said that was to the south, but did not mention it. The Grimm reverted to its animal form; this time, it was much more majestic, sporting the same grey and black fur, clean and straight. There was now an aura about it, almost a glow of warm light that would make you feel at peace. The light shone brighter for a moment, and the party flinched, only to find, after re-adjusting their eyes, that Death was gone.

The party, now left standing in a grassy field, remained quiet. Without a word, they decided to continue on their journey towards the Fractured Anvil. Continuing across the Kishar Grasslands to the edge of the woodlands, through the thick forest that the adventurer first traversed at the beginning of his journey. Leading the horses on foot through the dense tree population, the interaction with the one that called itself Death ever weighed on their minds.

Was what it said true? Could they trust it? It did carry a powerful presence of divinity about it. Was Pluteus right to be sceptical, was Nectarion to have faith in an unproven ally?

Along with the lightless forest, the cool, damp air at night around the fire still provided little warmth.

After six long, cold and dim days, the party began to see light ahead. They quickened their pace and broke through the tree line, and there it was. Standing before them was the tallest mountain that imagination could have ever conceived. Surrounded by what appeared to be farmlands as far as the eye could see, the base of the mountain was indiscernible, but the mountain itself was magnificent. Right down the centre, dividing the mountain into two spires of hard, black rock, was its namesake: The fracture with a light red glow at the base of the divide.

The party stood for the longest time in absolute awe. Nothing like this existed in Edron, and they had never seen the likes before. They looked at each other, took one another by the hand and gingerly but excitedly took the first step into a new world.

Chapter Eleven

As the companions made their way out of the forest, they were now in the open landscape, which looked to be farmland. A dirt road that bisected the different paddocks lay just before them, heading straight to the mountain and on the horizon, they could see its peak penetrating the blue sky.

They made their way slowly down the dirt road, and the party began to notice that these farmlands were very unusual. They saw fenced paddocks where crops would be, should be, yet what they saw instead was crop stubble, the withered remains of crops. One paddock near the road had the remains of beanstalks lying before them, dead pods and brittle vines covering the ground, lifeless and dull.

Another paddock showed the remains of what would have been cornamelon, and the further they walked, the more they saw of this blighted farmland. Nectarion stopped and crouched down near some of the dead crops to investigate, ascertaining that they died of natural causes, lack of water and care. The party then noticed that these farmlands were very quiet and empty. In the distance, they could see a farmhouse and began making their way towards it.

Upon reaching the front door, the group saw the front door ajar, cold air hung in the homestead, and it was dead quiet. It reminded them of the farmhouse they discovered at the beginning of their journey, which Orcs had raided. The party gingerly open the door fully to peer inside. The dark, dry, cool homestead produced a hint of a sour smell that lingered in the air. The party entered, and light from the doorway illuminated the home slightly, and they could see the inside.

A table and chairs sat in the centre of the room with a small kitchen area in the back. A bench for food preparation, with a window above it looking out on the fields and a cast-iron stove in the corner with an angled flue that exited through a hole in the wall. The home was 'L' shaped, and there was a door at the back of the abode off the kitchen area. Near the front of the house was a small living area featuring a wooden bench seat and a curtain that provided privacy for a small double bed.

As the party investigated the homestead, there didn't seem to be anything disturbed. The furniture remained in place and intact, and there were no signs of a struggle. The only clue was a plate of food that looked a few days old, remaining placed upon the table. Half-eaten, the grey fuzz of mould growing, and flies buzzed around it. It was as if whoever was here just got up and left, mid-dinner.

After finding nothing more to indicate what truly happened here, the group decided that there was nothing more to be gained and continued on their way down the dirt road. After a few more kilometres, things began to worsen when they came across the remains of livestock. Similar to what they saw in the Forest of Marr, the decayed remains of bovine and sheep filled the pasture where they once grazed.

As the party surveyed the scene, they noticed some individuals coming towards them, who seemed to be walking quite slowly and showed signs of possible injury as they walked with a limp. As a few moments passed, they could now see that the individual was not well. It was very obvious that their limbs were twisted and broken, and yet they still functioned as they limped towards the companions.

"I think we should keep moving", Nectarion expressed nervously.

The party picked up their pace a little and put some distance between them and the shambling people. As they made their way, they noticed another group of individuals coming towards them from the other direction and found themselves between two groups of potentially dangerous individuals.

With the two groups now closing the distance between them and the companions, they could see exactly what was wrong with them. Their jaws were dislocated, and their mouths were gaping open, and their eyes - there weren't any. Instead, there were bloody, hollow sockets where their eyes should be and dried blood tears underneath them. Their attire was that of common folk, workers. *Farmers*.

The party came to a halt and poised ready for an attack. Minny held her shield firmly, and Nectarion gripped his axe tight. Pluteus readied his staff, and Oophaga drew their broadsword, while Purvan stood fast. The shambling people came to the fence at the edge of the paddock and began to awkwardly climb through the wire, stumbling somewhat as they did.

Nectarion took his Hallowed axe and threw it at the adversaries in front of the party, slicing across the first and then the second, as it arced, leaving gaping wounds across the torso, before the axe swung around and returned to his hands.

"I count six!" Purvan shouted.

"Eight. There are two more over there closing in." Pluteus replied.

Minny went into a full charge at the shambling corpses behind the party, using her shield to knock down a fence post, continuing to plough into one of them. She then took her mace in hand and swung, making contact with another just next to her first target.

Oophaga locked their gaze on one of the corpses behind the party and cast Unleash Chaos upon it. The effect of the spell missed the corpse, and Ooph closed the gap between them, striking it with their broadsword. The corpse then directed its attention to Ooph and wounded them.

One of the corpses close to Minorha made a move on her; it attempted to maul and gnaw on Minny's shell to no effect. She turned to return the favour, and the hit caused little damage. They seem to be much hardier than they appeared.

Pluteus was engaged by another corpse only to dance around the attack and connect his Greatstaff with the creature, but it refused to cease and continued to encroach on him.

Nectarion embedded his axe into another, causing critical damage. As he removed the axe from the corpse's body, it incurred an even greater infliction and fell to the ground, a broken body all twisted and devoid of life. Standing next to Nectarion, Minny swirled around on the spot like a whirlwind and brought down another corpse, as it flew back several feet onto the ground, remaining there, still and lifeless.

The remaining corpses, now through the fence, surround the party. The threat was increasing somewhat. As one closed in on

Purvan, he let out a musical sound, and the party rallied together to finish this battle.

> *"All shamblin' undead scare the livin' shit out of me*
> *They could care less as long as someone'll bleed*
> *So darken your prose and strike a violent pose*
> *Maybe they'll leave us alone, but unlikely."*

Nectarion's axe came swinging around again, and another corpse went down as its head was separated from its body, tumbling through the air and dropping to the ground, rolling like a pumpkin before coming to rest.

Minny smashed another, using all her weight behind the attack and shattered the corpse; it fell to the ground in a heap of broken bones. With only three remaining, the party's spirits lifted; they could win this.

Ooph, still in combat with their adversary, swung their broadsword and missed. Minny, looking on at this, yelled to Ooph.

"Don't worry, Ooph, you'll get this, just keep trying!"

In their frustration, Ooph placed their frog-like hand upon the shambling corpse and cast Cinder Grasp.

"You're a naughty farmer."

A burst of flame erupted from their palm, and the corpse was ignited. In agony, the corpse ran past Ooph, through the other party members, slightly burning Purvan, Pluteus, Minny and one of its fellow corpses in the process and continued to sprint ineptly down the road, screaming and wailing.

With one corpse remaining, it began to act in fear and retreated from the battle. The party move forward, intimidating

165

their adversary. Minny burst forward from the group and smashed into the corpse, rebounding off her shield and hitting the fence post behind it, falling to the ground.

With the last of the attackers down, the party ensured there were no other threats and relaxed.

"I think we should amputate these things and then burn the remains, ensure that they aren't going to come back," suggested Nectarion.

"What do you think these things were?" Pluteus inquired.

"They seemed like zombies but didn't show the usual traits of a zombie," conjectured Purvan.

"They were definitely something of the undead variety, Nectarion is right. We should burn them," insisted Oophaga.

The companions gathered the corpses, cut their limbs and the heads from the torso and placed them in a heap. Ooph cast Cinder Grasp again to ignite the bodies. Waiting half an hour to guarantee that they were fully disposed of and that the fire didn't spread across the farmlands, the party then composed themselves once more and began to trek down the road as if it were just another normal day.

The rest of the day remained quiet and still. There was no sign of the corpse that had run away, blazing with fire, and the paddocks continued to show the same withered crops or deceased animals as before. The sun descended behind them, touching the trees of the forest that they had emerged from. The sky was sparse with a few clouds and slight hints of orange and purple glow off them. The party, tired, looked for a place to rest when the scene began to change, and the blighted farmlands of before turned green. Full-grown crops filled the paddocks, and an individual could be seen nearby.

Looking closely, the group determined that this individual was not one of those shambling corpses they had encountered before. They slowly approached and could see the individual approaching them. A Human man wearing similar attire to the corpses, and a straw hat that looks like the one Minny wore sometimes. His face was covered mostly in hair as his reddish-brown beard grew down to his chest, his brown eyes the only visible feature.

"Greetings, good sir, my friends and I are travelling through these lands of yours and are looking for lodgings, if there are any?" posed Nectarion to the stranger.

He took stock of the party, an interesting and peculiar group of people in his land and in a thick, rustic drawl, he answered.

"Ya' wanna be careful roun' these parts, nah much been goin' well for us folks."

In quick response with enthusiasm, Nectarion responded.

"We took care of those contaminated creatures some way back. Those former farmers are now laid to rest."

The farmer looked at the party more intensely and realised that they were some kind of fighters or warriors.

"Ya'll took 'em on?"

"Yes, we did," Minny confirmed.

"Well, ya'll better folla me, my place is just yonder and me missus, Lilly, be hav'en the dinna on by now." He collected his tools from nearby and led the party in the direction of his home, which could just be seen off in the distance.

"Me name's Bernard, but ya'll can juss call me Bernie."

The party then introduced themselves and began to regale their journey to Bernard.

Bernard and the party reached his homestead, and the door swung open abruptly.

"Lilly, I'm home, we got company wiff us, out-a towners."

A woman came from behind a wall, dressed in a simple, green, cotton dress with a white cotton apron. Dirty blonde hair done up and the pointed ears of an Elf, responded in a similar but sweeter voice than her husband's.

"Well, I be damned, we hav'en' had folks like this for quite a while," she pointed at Pluteus and continued, "I hav'en seen yah kind for some time now," then looking at Nectarion, "I naugh' seen your kind ever."

The party, now completely within the house, began to mill around the room until Lillian invited them to sit.

"Ya'll juss in time, I'm bout to serve up some grits and viddles for dinna."

The party did the best they could to find a place to sit. The smaller folk had no difficulty, but Minny, Pluteus and Nectarion, being somewhat larger, found it uncomfortable.

Lillian served up the dinner, and all partook in the evening meal. It is quiet at first until Bernard breaks the silence.

"Yah sayin' befor that you came looking for trade and frein'ship?"

"That is true, we are seeking to ally ourselves with other regions, cultures and such, and by *ourselves*, I mean our people.

Our leaders have given us diplomatic status to conduct talks with others." Purvan explained in some detail.

"When we entered these lands, we didn't know what to expect, but it definitely wasn't what we came up against," added Nectarion.

"Well, ya deff'nitly lucky, cause we phought we cleared out all dem creatures. We lost some good folks and the crops. It gunna be hard this nekk season with half 'un the stock pushin' up daisies."

A moment passed as Bernard stared at his plate on the table and continued,

"At the same time, we los' people, so maybe it won' affect us too bad."

"Do you know what is happening to your people?"

"Nah, really. The council at the moun'in say it's some kinda poison or disease, a curse or mag'cal attack. What I do know is that for near two momphs, people just stopp working the fields, feedin' the stock, they just got lazy."

The conversation came to an end, and the party helped Lillian clear the table and clean up, while Bernard sat in an armchair smoking a pipe, next to the small fireplace. Lillian, standing at the bench with Minny, turned to her and asked,

"Yah Galapa. The Synd'cate? When the lass time you be at the Anvil?"

Minny's face looked uneasy; the talk of Syndicate matters always made her uncomfortable.

"Actually, I've never been," she replied in a reserved, quiet tone.

Purvan's voice, raised over all others, announced.

169

"Bernie, Lilly, we thank you for your hospitality, but I believe it is time for us to depart and make for the mountain."

"Ya'll do no such thin. Ya'll lookin' for lodgings, and so we will accom'date."

"Yes, the lease we could do for ya'll riskin' ya lives earlier." Lillian included.

"The little 'uns can sleep up here in the house, but you big-folk will 'ave to sleep out in the barn. I'll show ya." and Bernard led them out.

As the farming couple and the party lay asleep, there came a slight rumble in the ground. Those in the barn could feel it and were startled awake. They got up to investigate the situation, and they could feel the rumble just as it ended. They exited the barn and looked around; all seemed still and fine in the night. Just then, they looked up and could see streaks of fire streaming across the starry sky. Some of them hit the ground nearby, off in the distance. They rushed to the farmhouse to check on the others when another rumble occurred under their feet. This one was a little bigger, and the party nearly lost their balance as they ran.

Inside the house, everyone was awake and seemed to be unharmed by the situation. The others enter from outside, and Bernard shouts.

"*Wee-ooo!* We got dem trem'rs again."

It ceases to shake the ground, and all settles.

"What did you say *again?* You've had them before?" Pluteus queried.

"Yup, started roun' bout same time as all the other shit."

"And the sky fire, the shooting stars?"

"*Shootin' Stars.* That one's a new one," informed Bernard.

All of them stepped outside and looked up, where they could still see a few streaks of fire shooting across the sky. They simply stood there for quite a while, enjoying the show, all the while the party felt that this could be something more, relating to something elsewhere, something elusive.

The morning sun hit the farmhouse as it began its climb. The others in the barn can smell the fragrance of cooking, the fumes of breakfast. They come to the house and can see Purvan and Ooph already prepping the table, Bernard in his chair with a pipe, waiting for his meal to be served. The meals were placed, and all sat down to eat.

"Ya'll wanna keep headin' down the road, it goes straight to the moun'in. Ya'll reach Cav'nshire first, the town built into the moun'in caves. The Council is up higher in Cressloff, but if ya wanna make really good friends, look for the Mages of Sigma."

"We thank you again for the food and the bed. Look after yourselves and try to stay safe out here. We will see if we can offer any help to these mages you speak of." Purvan graciously said for the whole party.

The companions saddle and mount their horse, wave goodbye to Bernard and Lilliana.

"Stay safe, Ya'll come back now, ya' hear," was the last thing the party heard Bernard say, as they trotted off towards the mountain.

As the distance between the mountain and the party closed, the large division in the mountain became more definitive. A large crevice that divided the upper mountain into two before coming together about the mid-section, a slight hint of a red glow emanated from the fracture.

Finally reaching the outskirts of the mountain base, the party noticed the built-up area of a township. As they looked up the mountain, just before the division, there was a large structure that was attached to the southern side of the mountain.

The township around the mountain base seemed to be more of a processing area. Here, the group could see the organisation, loading of carts and transporting them into the mountain.

The party didn't seem to warrant any attention as they rode up slowly between the commotion of the workers. They could see the entrance, a large opening in the side of the mountain. An enormous wooden ramp ascended from the outside and into the cavern, allowing the carts of goods to be taken inside.

The party continued through and towards the large ramp. With no question, they entered. Inside the caverns of the mountain was a vast town built inside the caves. All wooden structures built on stumps, wooden ramps assisted the food carts to gain access onto the wooden platform that was the streets of this town. Moving through the street, the companions noticed that there were many shops, market stalls, restaurants, boutiques and small cafes. It was quite sophisticated. Above them, they saw what provided the cavern with light. Hundreds of arcane orbs, floating in mid-air, each one glowed like a small sun, illuminating the caverns as if the sun were actually above.

Remembering the compass, Purvan retrieved it from his pack. It spun sporadically now, as if it couldn't find its direction. As the party studied the compass, Minny moved away from the main group to search for assistance, perhaps a guard. After a short while, she came to realise there were no guards and she was lost, unable to find her comrades. At that point, she could see Nectarion hovering above as he yelled out,

"Follow me, back this way!"

Minorha watched Nectarion from above while carefully making her way back through the crowd of citizens in this busy market palace. She caught out of the corner of her eye a few Galapa, definitely Syndicate. She remained cautious as she continued to make her way.

Returning to her friends, she saw them looking at an interesting but somewhat familiar sight. In this large town square, bustling with people, they saw a large, round stone platform in the centre. As they watched, people were stepping onto and off it, and as they did, they vanished or appeared.

"I don't think we are going to find any help here," Minorha said as she reunited with the others.

"Shall we?" Pluteus suggested, gesturing towards the platform.

They waited for the moment and stepped onto the teleportation platform. The party was whisked up, and in an instant of arcane flash, the scene in front of them changed. When the scene rematerialised before them, they had been teleported from Cavernshire to Crestloft.

As they stepped off the platform, they saw more shops, markets, and fooderies lining the walkway that curved to the shape of the mountain. From the outside, the structure built onto the side of the mountain looked shabby and poorly designed, haphazardly attached to the rock face, but in here, it was all refined and elegant. The wooden abodes and shop fronts were crafted from the finest lumber, with filigree carvings in almost everything. Magical lamps lined the walkway around this promenade, bringing warmth to the visage. Behind them were large rectangular-shaped openings with no glass and a raised barrier that continued around the edge for safety. Looking out and down on the landscape below, from here, the party could see the small dots of those below, entering the cavern up the large ramp.

The party began to look around and peruse the various wares at the different stalls. They found a few interesting items that they purchased, all while trying to find some indication of the Mage's location. After a short while, they met up again at the teleportation circle.

"Did you find anything?" Pluteus asked.

"Nothing", the party responded.

"Did anyone think to ask someone?" Minny looked at her friends, with confoundedness on her face.

She walked over to a nearby tiny market booth, with a single male Elf standing inside. Above the counter was a sign that said *'Shien's Quality Coin Purses'*.

"Excuse me, my friends and I are looking for the Mages. Do you know how I can reach them?"

"You're looking for mages?" he answered vaguely.

"Yes, mages, the Mages of Sigma."

"Oh, my apologies, yes, the Mages of Sigma. Do you have an appointment?"

Minny looked at him, miffed.

"No, I don't have an appointment."

"Well, everyone knows if you want to see the Mages, you need to make an appointment. As a Galapa, I assumed *you* would know."

"Could you just tell me how to find them, so that I might make an appointment?"

"If you continue down the promenade that way, you will eventually come across another, smaller teleportation platform, inside a small alcove, on the left. It will take you to the level that the mages are on."

Minny nodded her head in thanks and walked back towards her companions. From behind her, she heard the Elf shout.

"Hey, do you want to buy a coin purse? They're good quality!"

Minny continued without a backwards glance, returning to the group.

"Well, did you find out where to go?" asked Pluteus.

"Follow me, this way." The party followed Minorha as she led them.

The party found the smaller platform not far from the coin purse vendor, a sign indicating that the platform would teleport them to the level where they could find the Council Chambers and the mage's location. They stepped upon it, and just like before, a whirl of arcane energy engulfed them, and before them, the scene had changed once again.

This level was rather quiet; there was no one about, and the open windows that looked down to the ground were before them. As they stepped out and off the platform, they turned to look at the wall and could now see directional information. One direction pointed to where the Council Chambers would be, and the other to something called the Sigma Sanctum.

"Do you think that is where we'll find them?" Oophaga pointed out.

"Makes sense, in my opinion," responded Nectarion.

The party ventured down the walkway of this promenade until they reached a set of large, open wooden doors. As they entered the main hall of the sanctum, with a polished stone-tiled floor beneath their feet, they noticed twelve large wooden doors positioned equally around the circular room, not including the double-doored entrance they had just entered. Each was carved with images depicting mages casting spells, reading old books, or holding a sword and wand. There was also writing above the doors indicating where they led. The only exception was the door directly across the room. It was much larger and was painted red, and there were no carvings or writing.

As they stood, milling around the centre of the room, one of the doors opened and an individual exited into the entrance hall, a large thud filled and echoed through the hall as the door automatically closed behind him. The individual was wearing fine, dark-reddish robes, trimmed with silver and gold, which definitely indicated a magic user. It seemed that in most cultures, mages loved their robes. His short, thick hair was slicked back with oil, away from his eyes and behind his ears - *pointed ears*.

"Can I assist you at all?" he asked the party in a plummy accent as he noticed their presence.

The party regale the mage, Daten, with their travels and how they now find themselves before him.

"I am grateful that you have come all this way to assist us and form an alliance of some sort, but my fellow mages and I have been working on this issue for two months now and have not made any progress. I am not sure what it is that you think you could contribute?"

Behind Nectarion, Minny whispered something to him.

"That may be the case, but the dig site we visited had professional archaeologists and experienced scholars who couldn't work out a riddle till we came along. I assure you, we can be very resourceful," relayed Nectarion.

"I am unfamiliar with what type of people you are used to working with, but the Mages of Sigma are very wise and skilled practitioners of the arcane arts. We are not some backwater caster of simple tricks." Daten proclaimed in a somewhat condescending and proud tone.

Purvan came forth and revealed his sketch book with the images of the archway they discovered in the ruins, and asked Daten.

"My good sir, would you have ever come across this language?"

Daten took the book from Purvan and looked at the sketches attentively, his face dropping ever so slightly as he answered.

"I am familiar with this language, although I do not know how to read it. Have you ever seen this language before?"

"No, it is completely unknown to us; this is the first occurrence we have had."

"Well then, you must know that this is an ancient language, so ancient that it has not been spoken aloud since well before the Dawn Year. Even before the Dark Ages."

"What is it?"

"This is the language of the gods," Daten revealed in awe. He began to ramble quietly to himself about how fascinating this is and how he would love to explore these ruins.

"Daten!" Purvan yelled, bringing him back to the conversation.

"Daten, we can help your people here if you really want us to. We can't tell you the specifics of why, just take solace in knowing we can help. Even if it is a small, mediocre task to begin with." Nectarion entreated.

Daten looked at the party, his face showing the exhaustion, the worry and the need to find a solution. His entire demeanour now completely changed, and in a thick, rustic drawl,

"If ya wanna help, ya could go to the lib'ry and do sum readin'. Ya may find sumphin we missed the firs' time."

The party looked at him, shocked at the loss of his Highbourne accent. He realised his mistake and quickly corrected himself, actively coughing, as if to clear his throat.

"Ahem, Ahem, excuse me, my name is Daten and I am the Mage Master of Biomancy. Ahem, welcome to the Sanctum, Ahem."

"What the hell was that?" Purvan questioned, containing a laugh, his companions following suit.

"Please forgive me, I must have had a dry throat, all this talking."

"How come you sounded like a farmer?" Ooph asked. "You sound like Bernie."

"You know Bernie, as in Bernard?" Daten inquired, surprised, and now talking like a Highbourne again.

"And his wife Lillian?"

"Yeah, we met them on the way here, took us in for the night and gave us a meal."

A look of relief fell across Daten's face as he straightened up again, standing tall.

"Look, if you really want to help, you can start in the lib-Crest Bibliotheca. The great archives of Crestloft."

The party readjusted itself to a more serious persona after the brief moment of jest.

"Once you have acquired several outcomes that you feel are viable, then return here and ask for *me* personally. I will be able to present you to the others."

The companions all nodded towards Daten, with respect for his position and the current situation he and his people were facing.

"We'll do what we can."

Chapter Twelve

After spending the night in an unused apartment in Crestloft, the party woke, fully rested. They bathed, had a hearty morning meal and dressed in their freshly cleaned clothes. The goal of today was for Pluteus, Purvan and Ooph to visit the Crest Bibliotheca, the great library here in Crestloft for which they had initially travelled. All the while, Nectarion and Minorha were going to head back to Bernard and Lillian's farm and search for the crash site of one of the falling stars.

Nectarion and Minny had ventured back down to Cavernshire, where the horses had been stabled. Minny mounted her bulking war steed, a necessity to carry her weight and the two headed out. Travelling back through the farmlands was like a pleasant day out. The green of the pastures and the crops in full growth.

They could see Bernard and Lillian's homestead in the distance and remembered the direction of one of the possible sites, and turned off the road across one of the pastures. Crossing the paddock of green grass, a few cattle in the distance here and there, they arrived at a crater with an impact trail stretching several meters behind, where a large black rock sat in the centre of the bottom.

"How far down do you think that is?" Minny asked.

"I would say no more than thirty feet. Hang on, I will fly you down so you don't slip."

Nectarion grabbed Minny under her muscular turtle arms and slowly hovered down into the crater. At a closer look, the rock wasn't black but a deep, dark yellow with scorch marks covering the majority of the surface, most likely from the fire that engulfed it as it fell from the sky two nights ago. At this distance, a pungent, foul, rotting smell filled their nostrils.

"What is that stench?"

"I don't know, but it smells like rotten eggs." Minny detested.

"Can you feel that as well? It feels warm."

As they got closer, they could see heat haze coming off the large stone. Stretching their hands out slowly, they placed a hand each in close proximity to the boulder and could feel the heat emanating from it.

"It fell two nights ago and is still warm." Nectraion pointed out.

Without a second thought, Minorha took out her mace and slammed it onto the rock. A shudder vibrated through the solid timber and into her arms, the stone still perfectly intact. She paused for a moment and put her weapon aside.

"I am going to see if I can lift it."

The rock, being about the size of a cart wheel and not entirely a perfect sphere, Minny felt she could pick this up quite easily. Nectarion moved in, deciding to aid her. As they lifted it, they were quite surprised by its lack of weight, being extremely light for what they had depicted.

"I feel like I could pick it up with one hand." Minny gloated.

"Do you feel that, though? It's extremely warm, it's actually starting to burn"

They both dropped the rock and could feel the heat in their palms still lingering.

"What do you think we should do?" asked Minny.

Nectarion looked at the situation,

"If we can lift it quickly, we may be able to secure it to the horse, on the saddle. That should be enough to protect it from being burnt. I think we need to take this back to our good friend Daten for analysis."

Like a couple of crabs carrying the rock up the side of the crater awkwardly, Minny tried not to slip back down the dirt while Nectarion buzzed above the ground. Just as they neared the rim of the crater, they threw the rock up into the air, waiting for the thud of impact. They clambered to the surface and slowly crawled out.

"That was fun," Minny said with a layer of sarcasm.

"It's all about staying fit; you never miss rock-throwing day."

The two rested a moment and caught their breath before Minny picked up the rock and balanced it on the saddle of her horse. The beast startled for a moment until she settled him, trying to assure him that he would be fine. Nectarion took out his sceptre, which is adorned with the skull of his murdered queen and used the nectar to coat a couple of ropes.

"That should help, buy us some time, so the heat from the stone doesn't burn them out."

With that, the two head back to the road and towards the mountain.

****

The room was quite large and circular. The Bibliotheca was built into the mountain, which was one of the most difficult projects, as the composition of the rock was very unique and difficult to cut. The walls were hewn but quite smooth, and around the perimeter of the room were tall bookshelves, separated by imitation windows in the rock wall, with the same glowing orbs that light the caverns of Cavernshire, behind the glass. The shelves were so tall that a catwalk was built all the way round, with access via ladders to reach the higher books. In the centre of the room was a circular booth with two access points for the library attendees, and like a flower in full bloom, large, solid wooden tables and benches spread out around the centre for patrons to sit and read.

Sitting at one of these tables, Purvan gave the appearance of a child of ten sitting at the 'grown-up's table, various tomes spread across the surface, some closed, some open, and his face buried in one of them, reading intently. Every now and then, he stops to take notes in his notebook or to sketch something. They had discovered large charts that depict a continent, parts of which look like Edron and the region where the Fractured Anvil is located, called Lacacia.

Pluteus returned to the table with another tome, this one about different legendary items and weapons. He opened it to a particular page and showed it to Purvan.

"That looks just like the chain shirt we find in Deimos. Siriana was right, it *is* a legendary Item."

Armour of Ruin - *chainmail that is said to bring ruin to those who attack its wearer. It is explained that those who attack its wearer have met untimely and odd demises. One incident depicted was during combat with the wearer, the assailant attacked, stepped back and was bludgeoned to death by a tree log that had rolled past where there were no trees for miles. The story continues to say that the log rolled down the nearby hill from an outcrop of trees being felled by lumberjacks, three miles away.*

"What a fascinating item. By the way, I was reading this book and discovered that there used to be a city in those grasslands we travelled through. According to this, it was in the far northern region."

Pluteus looked at Purvan, dumbfounded,

"I've already explained this to all of you; we already know about it. We met their descendants in the village of Afen, the *Elvish* people. You even laid with the seraph of the town, as you do."

"Why do you suppose we don't remember, and you do?"

"I don't know, but of all the times to not write in your notebook....... Maybe you were distracted?"

Another tome that they had been perusing contained different languages and dialects, most of which they knew. Ancient runes and modern-day languages. One entry, though, sparked interest. The language of the Gods, Enochian, which Purvan had been looking for. Now he could attempt to translate the script they had discovered on the arch in the ruins.

Oophaga, on the other hand, had spent their time investigating the origins of the Adventurer's journal with the initials K.D. One of the attendees was very helpful and gave Ooph a cup of tea while they waited for the attendee to return with any information.

When they did, they showed Ooph a record of expeditions undertaken over the last eight hundred years, including the Adventurer's. His name was Kester Dickory. He set out to find other settlements, as it had been several hundred years since there was contact with other people of the realm. Older records indicated a period after the Dawn Year when people who had settled in the region of the Fractured Anvil had come from far-off places. There was even an item ticket accompanying the record, which the attendee retrieved; the partner of the compass held by the party.

After spending the majority of the day in the library without a break, the companions decided to take a break. Oophaga and Pluteus volunteered to go get something to eat, while Purvan stayed behind, copying notes from the tomes to his personal journal.

****

On returning to the mountain, Nectarion and Minorha could see the sun beginning to nestle behind the far-off farmlands on the horizon. The day had passed by, and they were somewhat exhausted from walking back. The horse had had its fill of lugging this stone tied to its back, the rope almost spent as the hardened nectar had practically deteriorated. They decided not to carry the rock into Cavernshire and up to Crestloft, but instead, led the horse onto the transport platform and exited onto the promenade of Crestloft. No one minded their actions in Cavernshire as horses were a common sight in the town, but as soon as they appeared with a large animal on the promenade, many eyes became fixed on the two. Showing no concern for the onlookers, they continued on to the Sigma Sanctum, arriving shortly thereafter.

They entered the main hall of the Sanctum and approached the door that Daten had previously exited the day before. Minny gave a loud knock on the door, but received no reply. Unsure of what to do next, the two of them simply waited in the main hall quietly, with a large, peculiar rock on the back of a horse. Nectarion turned to Minny,

"Perhaps I should see how the others have fared in their endeavours?"

"Yeah, that's fine, I'll wait here until someone comes along."

"Yeah, that's no problem?"

"No problem at all."

Then Nectarion left the Sanctum in search of his friends.

Not long passed when an individual exited one of the other doors, another male Elf in his fine attire walked but a few steps when he noticed what was before him.

"Where are you taking this…..thing?" He queried.

"I am here to meet with Daten, he told me to come back if we had found anything of interest."

"Daten? Fair enough, please wait here," and he approached the door that led to Daten's whereabouts, simply pushing it open as he entered. He threw a comment to Minorha over his shoulder.

"Just so you know, if that animal leaves any surprises, you will be cleaning it up," he said in a stern voice, and the door slammed shut behind him.

Momentarily, the door opened again, and the previous mage returned, followed closely by Daten.

"Ah, you have returned. What is this?" Daten was staring at the horse.

"*This* is a large rock we found out in the farmlands. This is what landed a couple of nights ago when we saw the fire in the sky."

Both Daten and his associate inspected the stone on the horse's back.

"Be careful, there is a heat emanating from it that could burn you." Minny cautioned.

187

Both mages waved their hands in arcane gestures.

"What do you think, Respen?"

"I am unfamiliar with its composition, it has a foul odour about it and the heat……"

He trailed off in thought before he continued.

"Do you believe this to be linked to the current situation?"

"I will have to conduct more thorough tests," Daten concluded.

Daten waved his hands again, and the almost burnt ropes came loose as he began to levitate the stone towards his door.

"I guess I will return to my own studies," Respen announced.

"Yes, of course. Oh, Respen, could you get someone to take care of the horse? My apprentice is unavailable at the moment."

Daten continued with the levitating stone, and Minorha followed behind him. Respen's eyes just rolled back as he entered his own door.

****

Nectarion entered the large depository of tomes. Not many patrons were here, and noticing Purvan was easy. Still sitting at the wooden desk, taking notes and reading.

"How have you been?"

Purvan looked up and noticed his large bee-like friend.

"I do believe I am all 'booked' out. I couldn't read another word."

"Where are the others?"

"Went to get some food. Ah, here they are now,"

Oophan and Pluteus entered the library carrying containers filled with food. The four of them sat and ate, leaving Minny something to eat. A Galapan delicacy that the others had tried and enjoyed. Pieces of meat, covered in rice and wrapped in a paper-thin, green substance. The party did not bother to ask what it was made of; they chose to be adventurous.

Afterwards, they made their way back to the Sigma Sanctum to rejoin Minny and discover what revelation Daten may have found.

"So the large rock you located in the farmlands is what is called sulphur, or brimstone, which is the common term. The interesting thing about this find is that no one I am aware of has ever found such a large, concentrated deposit. It develops naturally, underground and yet this was one of many that fell from the sky, engulfed in fire."

"So what does that mean? What do flaming rocks of fire falling from the sky, dead crops, earthquakes, and the undead all have in common?" Pluteus blurted out in frustration.

Daten looked at the party, wishing he had the answers,

"I have absolutely no idea," he replied, disheartened. "Look, it is late and we are all tired. Perhaps we should retire for the evening and resume in the morning with fresh minds?"

The party agreed and said good night to Daten, returning to their loaned abode.

The group sat in their apartment, not entirely ready for bed, going over notes and discussing the particulars of their findings and trying to connect the dots. After a few tedious and painstaking hours had passed, they had no results until Purvan jumped up in excitement.

"What, what is it? Ooph asked ecstatically.

"An idea, a theory. Wait here, I will be back shortly."

His friends looked annoyed with the lack of information as Purvan just upped and ran out the door.

Another hour passed before Purvan returned with yet another book in his hand.

"This is it, this is the connection."

Opening and reading a passage from the book he had brought, entitled *'Great Prophesies and Future Events'*

> *As the sky falls and the earth trembles,*
> *The sun will turn as dark as sackcloth,*
> *The moon will be as red as blood,*
> *The oceans will boil, and the lands will decay*
> *Corruption will cover the world*
> *The Seven will be shattered*
> *And the Domains of Darkness will again walk the lands.*

A small but very clear word was spoken by the short frog-person, breaking the silence that had fallen in the room.

"Shit."

Chapter Thirteen

The entrance hall to the Sigma Sanctum had been slowly filling over the course of the last hour. The group and Daten had met earlier that morning with their findings from the previous evening. Daten, too, was shocked at the revelation of the connection. He wasted no time in summoning the department heads of the different schools of magic.

Respen had arrived first with two others, a female Elf named Jastira, Master of Abjuration and a female Human named Bellas, the Supreme Magistrate of Law on the Anvil Council. The room continued to fill, an array of mages in various designs of attire, but all sporting red. The party and Bellas seemed to be out of place at this gathering of arcane alumni.

"All right, Daten, we are all here now. What is the meaning of this? There are important works to be done." The chamber echoed with the voice of a female Drakonan.

"Yes, Lakku, we are getting to that. As we all know, these past few months have been trying times for us and our people. The outer farmlands have suffered, and we have not just lost crops and livestock, but good people. As you are aware, two nights ago, we experienced another quake, luckily with no loss. But a new phenomenon occurred. Fire fell from the sky, what has been colloquially referred to as a firestorm among the masses."

"Yes, yes, we know all this, get on with it." A male Halfling shouts from the back, hidden in the crowd of red, behind a few others.

"The arrogance in here is so thick, you could cut it with a broadsword," Purvan whispered to Ooph.

"Until this morning, we have had no viable solution to the issue, and I believe we won't find one, not in the conventional sense. Thanks to a group of newfound friends, it has come to my attention that we may be dealing with something on a much grander scale. I believe we are looking at the early warning signs of an apocalypse."

The room became filled with murmurs and small talk as the mages all turned to one another.

"I told you, I said it. I knew there was something much more than a blight or curse. The end times are near." Yelled another male Human above the chit-chat.

"Surely this can't be true?" Respen queried. "Has this something to do with that rock?"

"What rock?" another asked.

"Yesterday, my associates brought to me a large rock that was comprised solely of brimstone. It is what fell from the sky. And don't call me Shirley."

A moment passed with more talk amongst the mages when Daten revealed the tome that was given to him by the party and read aloud the passage shown to him by Purvan.

"So it would seem, Jadon was on the correct path in assuming something darker was at play," acknowledged Daten, looking at the male Human across the room.

Bellas stepped forward,

"On behalf of the council, I would ask, if there is no solution to this problem, what *is* it we can do?" Her soft voice seemed to carry throughout the hall with a texture of firmness, a look implying that the mages needed to find one.

"My associates and I have discovered additional information on items of power that may be the answer." Disclosed Daten, while looking at Respen, now standing together with Lakku and Jadon, gave a pointed look of acknowledgment.

"What items do you speak?" Lakku questioned, looking for verification.

"Crystals. Said to contain immense power."

The faces of all the mages in the room sank a little.

The assembled mages had been talking amongst themselves for the better part of an hour, discussing and processing the new information.

An apocalypse, this can't be. How will we overcome this? I'd better go and see my folks before we die.

Respen, Lakku and Jaden approached Daten and his associates.

"Daten, can we have a moment of your time?" Lakku gestured to a spot that was away from the bulk of the crowd.

"What do you think that is all about?" asked Pluteus, curiously.

A few moments passed, and the four mages returned to the party.

"When this meeting is adjourned, there is something that we have agreed that you should see," Daten informed them, a slight glimmer of intrigue and excitement in his eyes.

Once the meeting had been concluded, it did not take long for the assembly to disband and go about their business, disappearing behind the various doors in the hall. Daten, Respen, Lakku, Jadon and the party now remained. The mages looked at the party and then at the large red door across the way and motioned towards it. The four mages pressed their hands to it and initiated an arcane charge from their palms. The doors made a loud clonk and opened inward.

The mages led the party through the red door to an antechamber and closed the doors behind them. The walls are beautifully decorated with images of the gods in all their glory during the Forgotten Times. Lakku went over to the wall and pushed a panel inwards. A loud clonk noise echoed through the room, and the floor opened up to reveal a spiral stone stairwell, descending down into the dark.

The mages, followed by the party, descended the stairs, and magical sconces lit up along the walls as they did. They reached the bottom and found a small cavern made of the same black rock as the mountain. Further on, a tunnel that led to an old mine railway with very unique-looking carts. They had been modified to cater for humanoid passengers.

The companions looked on as the mages entered the carts.

"Are you coming?" Respen queried.

They entered the carts after the mages, Daten, and Minny sat in the rear cart, while the rest of the party managed to fit in one, and the other three mages occupied the front cart.

"I suggest you use the safety straps; these things can gain some speed. We have even clocked one going eighty-eight kilometres an hour," explained Jadon.

The carts started to roll forward, running on some kind of arcane propulsion, and they really did begin to pick up speed. As they were propelled along the tunnel, beacons of light illuminated ahead for several metres, not that there was much to see; it was all just rock, the inside of the mountain.

After travelling for about twenty minutes, the carts began to slow and they finally came to a complete stop at just the right moment, halting at a rock platform. The group stepped out onto the platform, the rock cavern turning into a crafted stone floor that led to a large archway. Sconces lit up the cavern as they approached. Through the archway and down a small corridor, a large chamber opened up, and the cavern was lit up with more sconces all around the walls.

"Welcome to the heart of the mountain," Respen announced, "They say this is where the gods crafted items of such power and legendary status."

He pointed to the centre of the room where a dais sat, and centred upon it was a large, one-foot-tall crystal with a light red glow.

"This is the Sigma Crystal; this is where the Mages of Sigma gain the extensive power and wisdom. It talks to us and guides us and has even told us the history of the gods, which we recorded and have in the Bibliotheca." Respen continued, waving his hand, and magery appeared around the room.

"In the beginning, the gods, colossal-sized creatures, walked amongst the mortals in peace, teaching us and helping us grow. Their mother, who could not walk amongst us, lived in the

*Heavenly Halls where her children would visit and tell her of their
adventures.*

*Then the Rupture came, and the world was broken. The
gods had to leave to fight a great evil, a great serpent of immense
proportion, a world-eater.*

*Afterwards, the mortals were left to tend to the realm
themselves, which was thousands of years ago.*

*The crystal says that the gods gave up their divinity and
became the first giants in the world and that modern giants are
descended from them."*

Pluteus and Purvan, intrigued by the crystal, approached it.
They placed their hands on it, and it lit up, much brighter. The red
glow filled the cavern. Touching it, it activated, the crystal began
to separate, and smaller parts of the crystal came away from the
main core and began to levitate around the core. Suddenly, a red
beam shot upwards, and a small orifice in the cavern roof allowed
the beam to continue.

Illusory visions filled the space above the crystal.

They saw a giant of a man with one eye hammering on an
anvil that looked just like the mountain, except without the
fracture. The weapon he was working on looked like a greatsword
or broadsword.

Another vision, an army of foul, vile beasts walked across
the land, following a tall, striking figure with a blend of diabolical
and handsome features. Devilish in appearance with horns, claws,
and wings, contrasted with a charming or unnerving smile. He had
a handsome face, long black hair, and piercing eyes that were dead

white. His attire included flowing capes and elegant robes, adorned with jewels, reflecting his status as a powerful being.

Finally, images of six other crystals that surrounded the red one on the dias, a yellow, an orange, a blue, a purple, a green and a white.

The moment passed, and the shards rejoined the core crystal, returning to its previous state.

"It's never done that before," Jadon spoke, a shocking tone in his voice.

The nine of them exited the large red doors and entered the entrance hall once more. The experience of what just happened heavily lay on all of them. The mages had never witnessed such a thing, nor had anything ever been recorded since the Sigma Mages had originally found the Sigma Crystal over a thousand years ago. Respen addressed the party.

"All we can suggest is to wait. I know it's the worst thing to say, but until we can ascertain what these visions mean or when they will happen, we are somewhat useless."

"We do thank you for what you have done. You have presented us with something that is at least viable to work towards. It seems even the wisest need a little help now and then." Lakku said graciously.

"Luckily, I have made some progress in my studies, so perhaps it won't take as long." Added Jadon.

"What will you do now?" Daten asked the party.

"We don't know exactly?" Necatarion dishearteningly said. "It's kind of difficult to know what to do when you've discovered that it all could be gone tomorrow."

"Sometimes the best thing to do is nothing. We just have to go through the motions and see what *that* tomorrow brings us."

"Very true, Jadon, very true," Daten commented.

Depressed and glum, the five companions sat at one of the food vendors on the promenade. They had ordered food for lunch, but none of them had really touched their meals. In the cacophony of the midday hustle of the crowd, a chime could be heard like the sound of a sweet chirping bird. The friends all looked at each other in a haze of confusion until Purvan realised it was coming from him. The Speaking Orb. He removed it from the pouch and held it in his open hand.

"Hello, is this thing on? Can you hear me?" Came a familiar, pitched, raspy voice the party knew well.

"Stellda? Is that you?" Purvan asked

"Of course, it's me, who else would it be? Look, there isn't much time. I have contacted you to inform you that the former queen's sister of Aurisolis has deposed her niece and taken the throne." The party looked at Nectaion as she said this. His face washed over with fury as he ran one of his four hands over the skull on his sceptre.

"There's more. About a week or so ago, the Hall of Mages was broken into, and four Omega Clone Crystals were taken. There were no witnesses or clues left. We believe the two are connected."

The party's attention was undivided as they listened to Stellda intensively.

"Last report I heard, the Apis-Military had marched on Goshan and made camp on the northern perimeter. They have issued an ultimatum, and your friend Lord Hobo has twenty-four hours to surrender."

"What if they don't?" Nectarion desperately inquired.

"Then they will enter the city by force and seize control."

"Why is she doing this? What is her goal?" asked Ooph.

"No one entirely knows. She has been dubbed *The Mad Queen* due to her irrational actions. If it was she who was responsible for the theft of the crystals, it's possible that the power from them has corrupted her?"

"Oh, she is just *bat-shit* crazy," Nectarion stated. "What about Mellivara, Espirette's niece?"

"As far as we are aware, she is still alive, just incarcerated."

"Where are you, Stellda?" asked Purvan.

"I am still in Westhold. Lord Hobo sent word of his situation and asked for aid, which seems pointless because the city guards of all the cities put together couldn't face the Apis-Military."

"That is correct. If not by sheer numbers, the elite warriors of the hive are more than a match for the handful of mediocre soldiers of Edron," assured Nectarion. "We have but one option that will be viable to lessen the carnage and loss. If we can remove the Mad Queen and put Mellivara back on the throne, she will be able to signal the military to halt and return to the hive. There is really nothing we can do in Goshan except help a handful of people escape. Unless the Lord Governor surrenders, but I doubt he will. He is not prepared for such."

The others all looked at their bee-like friend.

"We are with you. We know you have been searching for her since we met." Pluteus said in a comforting tone, placing his Fungril hand on Nectarion's shoulder.

"Stellda."

"What?" she replied abruptly.

"If you can get word to Lord *Obo* to hold off as long as possible, we will attempt an incursion into the hive in Aurisolis and take back control of the military," explained Purvan.

"Where are you now?"

"We are at the Fractured Anvil."

"Oh, that's fantastic. Where the hell is that? Do you expect me to know everything? Just cause I'm a sage and three hundred years old, I am supposed to be the *all-seeing* know-it-all."

Purvan rolled his back and continued.

"It's a place in the far north, very far, far away."

"Well, how are you going to get to Aurisolis in time, if you are very far, far away?"

At that statement, the party all looked at each other, hoping someone had an idea.

The loud sound of the door swinging open abruptly startled Daten out of his chair, and he fell to the ground behind his desk. The party had burst into his study and began shouting.

"We need your help! We need a teleportation platform that can send us a great distance." Blurted out Nectarion.

Daten led the party back out of his study, through the entrance hall, and entered another door across from his. The engraving on the wooden door depicted a symbol that resembled something to the effect of teleportation. Inside, there was a room, very similar to the one in Goshan, with a few differences.

To the side, a device was embedded into the wall with a round metal ring. A square stone jutted out from the wall with an indent of a hand.

"Place your hand here, and think about a location," instructed Daten. "Now, because there is no platform where you are going, no anchor point, this trip is going to be highly unpredictable. There is no telling where you will exit the stream. You could end up under the ground or in the middle of a wall or not even rematerialise at all. Are you sure you want to risk it?"

Nectarion looked to his friends for their support and back to Daten

"We do."

Nectarion placed one of his hands on the stone, and an image of Aurisolis appeared in the metal ring. The party stepped on the platform, and just like the teleporter in Goshan, it lit up with a magical barrier, and each of them was converted into energy and teleported. A moment of bluish arcane energy filled their sight, and then the room around them changed from the Sigma Santum at the Anvil to the interior of the palace in Aurisolis.

Above them, they could see the throne room suspended via supports made of petrified bees' wax. An unusual energy emanating from it. Drones flew all around in commotion, and far above, in the ceiling, was an opening for the drones to enter and exit.

Once more, the companions readied themselves to fight. But this time, the biggest confrontation they will have ever faced.

Chapter Fourteen

On the edge of the Northern Orchard Forest was the kingdom of Aurisolis, home of the Apis-fae. The only known subspecies of Faerie to have its own state. The main city sat above ground, but the full extent of the kingdom, the hive, where nectar, wax and other various commodities are developed, existed underground.

The Apis-fae provided an important element to the overall community of Edron, as the female drones are charged with the pollination of the Orchard Forest. This generated stronger and greater yields for harvest than those in a natural scenario and reduced the risk of famine for all denizens in Edron.

The surface city was a magnificent visage of structures, built with petrified bees' wax, an extremely strong and hard form of the wax that the hive developed. The city's main purpose was to welcome neighbouring kingdoms to visit without entering the hive.

The crowning jewel of the city was the main palace, situated within the centre and standing tall above all other buildings at forty stories. The internal structure was open and hollow.

Inside, the party stood where they rematerialised and saw at the top of the palace that the ceiling had openings that allowed drones to exit and enter the palace. The palace was busy with drones flying about, and there was a commotion around the throne room. An unusual, arcane energy surrounded the chamber.

The throne room was a spherical chamber, a hundred and fifty feet wide and made of honeycomb, suspended in the midsection of the building via beams of the petrified wax.

Nectarion whispered to his companions.

"We are exposed here, but it seems we have gone unnoticed thus far. I think we should find Mellivara first and get her to safety."

"We are with you, friend, lead the way," Ooph said comfortingly.

"Wait, before we go." Purvan halted the party.

Don't stop us now
We're havin' such a good time, havin' a ball
Don't stop us now
If you wanna have a good time, let's just kill 'em all
'Cause we're havin' a good time
Don't stop us now
Yes, havin' a good time
We're going to end this bitch after all, yeah.

His friends looked at him with a weird smile as their spirits were lifted and they gained a renewed sense of piety.

On the floor of the palace were four large openings being guarded by drones.

"Over there, those lead down into the hive and where they would most likely be holding Mellivara, in the prison block."

"Nectarion, it's guarded. I doubt we will make it past them easily," Pluteus mentioned with concern.

"True. And I don't want anyone to be harmed if we can help it. The drones are just following orders."

"I have an idea," stated Purvan and moved a few steps forward. Raising his hand slightly, he cast Mysterious Mist, and a cloud of thick fog surrounded the nearest group of guards and the entrance.

"There, now they can't see us."

"Yes, but we can't see them either." Pluteus pointed out.

"It will have to do, let's move." Nectarion led the party across the way to the fog.

They saw the large, shadowy figures of the guards, and knowing the entrance to be just in front of them, they crouched down to the floor and slid down into the hive. The drop from the entrance was about twenty feet, and the party had to be careful not to stumble and arouse the guards. As they made it to the next level, Nectarion remembered.

"Wait here, in the chamber." He instructed them. "I will return momentarily."

His comrades waited for a few moments until he came buzzing quietly back into the room, holding three strange devices that looked like wings.

"Here, put these on. We issue these to visitors when they come to the city. They are wing harnesses. Once you have donned them, they will be able to form a psychic connection for control. All you have to do is think 'fly' or 'up' and you should be able to hover like me."

"There are only three." Minny iterated.

"I know. I will carry you, Ooph, as you are the lightest."

The group slowly and surely made their way down through the hive, cleverly dodging patrols as they did. The prison block was located halfway down in the hive, underground. Made of honeycomb, the cells had hexagonal bars constructed from the petrified wax and enchanted with magic to be unbreakable. They reached the prison block untested and found Mellivara to be the only detainee. Nectarion approached her cell and bowed.

"My Queen, I have come to rescue you."

"Nectarion, is that you?"

"Yes, my Queen."

"Where have you been? It's been months since I sent you on your mission."

"Yes, my Queen. Unfortunately, I found no solid leads."

"How do we get her out, Nectarion?" asked Minny.

"Check the Warden's office, there should be an arcane key shaped like a hexagon about the size of this," and he pointed to a slot in the cell door where the key would go.

"I must retake the throne; my aunt has gone too far. If we don't hurry, the drones will attack Goshan for sure."

"My Queen, I understand the urgency to reclaim the throne and bring this ordeal to an end, but I must insist that your safety at this moment is paramount. We must get you to safer quarters before we confront Espirette."

"You're right, my good friend. Where shall we go?"

"I can take you to my residence. It is well secured, and no one will suspect looking for you there. We must make haste, though."

Minny approached the cell and handed the hexagonal key to Nectarion, and he placed it in the slot, releasing the arcane lock and opening the cell door.

"We'll have to disguise her somehow. We can't have her being noticed." Purvan said.

"I have another idea."

Nectarion removed a large, black cloth from his pack and began to coat it with his honey reserves. He then placed the cloth over the Queen like a cloak, obscuring her appearance.

"This won't just mask her appearance but her scent as well."

"It is an older technique, but it should work," Mellivara commented.

"Now quickly, my residence is not far from the palace, but we still need to be cautious."

The sound of the door unlocking echoed in the empty apartment. Nectarion's residence had been left unattended for about four months now. He slowly cracked the door open and peered inside for any danger. Seeing that it was empty and just how he left it, he opened the door fully and entered, allowing the rest of the party and Mellivara to enter.

"You will be safe here, I promise. When we leave, lock the door with this."

He handed her a key similar to the one used in a prison cell.

"Stay low and quiet, and when I have completed my mission, I will return for you."

She looked at him with pride and sincerity, her many Apis eyes reflecting an iridescent shine.

"Good luck, my friend." They both smiled with emotion, and Nectarion joined his companions outside the residence as the door closed behind him.

Making their way back towards the palace, above ground, they passed patrols and troops moving through the streets of Aurisolis. They ducked in and out of buildings and side streets, avoiding detection all the way. Standing just outside the palace, very near where they first materialised, they could see one of the entrances to gain access.

"When we get inside, we should act casual. I will escort you up to the throne chamber and inform the guards that you are a diplomatic envoy, each representing your people." Nectarion instructed.

"Understood," they responded.

Just as he ordered, the party followed Nectarion back into the palace, casually. Once inside the great hollow structure, drones still buzzing around, he and the others lifted off the ground, Ooph in Minorha's arms, ascending higher to the chamber that housed the throne room. Nectarion halted at the entrance and addressed the guards, who had crossed their lances, barring entry.

"State your business." He ordered.

"I am Nectarion, Cleric of the Eternal Order, the Golden Sting, and I have come to stand before the Queen and present these individuals from our neighbouring kingdoms."

"Nectarion. I remember you. Did you not leave the hive some time ago?" The other guard queried.

"That is true. I was on a diplomatic mission to discuss relations with other nations, and I have now returned. So if you will be so kind as to grant me access to see our Queen, that would be much appreciated." Nectarion presented his royal seal, as his voice reached a somewhat pompous tone.

Sure of his authority, the guards removed their lances and allowed him and the party access to the throne room.

Inside the spherical chamber, there are no floors or walls per se. A catwalk from the entrance they had just passed through continued to a platform that fell just short of the actual throne. Another intersected it crossways from one side to the other. A terrace curved around the far side of the chamber where the throne of the Queen sits centralised, made from petrified bees wax and ornate gems. Sitting there, Espiritte, the former Queen Aurianna's sister and Mellivara's aunt. High and mighty above all, and appearing complacent.

Off to the sides and stationed around the room are her personal guards, six of them, but not the usual male drones of the hive. These were a different form of Faerie; they were Vespi-Fae. Anthropomorphic wasps, very similar in appearance to the Apis-Fae and their sworn enemies.

Nectarion had now come to realise how she gained a foothold in the hive and how she managed to dispose of her own sister. The Vespi-Fae are well known for their assassination skills. The party halted mid-way between their exit and the throne, as Nectarion continued to the end of the catwalk, his wing speed increasing slightly as fury rose within, stood on the platform and addressed the *Mad Queen*.

"I am here to end your reign after the death of my Queen. I am here to exact my revenge. Taste my blade and let it be the last. You will not escape like you did last time."

"You fools, you will not defeat me. I have power beyond any of you." With that, she stood from the throne, laughing maniacally, signalling her guards to make ready to attack. They became aggressive and moved in towards the party and Nectarion, wasting no time, striking at him first.

Now, standing right behind him, Nectarion's comrades had readied themselves. Minny gripped her mace in one hand and shield in the other.

Two of the Vespi-Fae aimed to attack Nectarion, and without hesitation, Minny placed herself in the line of fire, taking the damage from the first and turning to take damage from the second. Her hard shell provided some protection.

With his Hallowed axe in his hand, a golden glow of divine energy emanated from Nectarion as we swung his axe at the attacking Vespi-Fae, each of them quickly moving out of range as they took to the air and hovered just short of Nectarion's axe. He then encroached on the retreat, swinging again. This time, he hit his marks and caused them severe wounds across their abdomens, ending them instantly as they fell to the bottom of the throne chamber, lifeless.

Vengeful, Nectarion flew over to the terrace and landed just metres from the throne and the *Mad Queen,* wings buzzing with righteous fury.

The remaining four guards moved on the party's position, two to the side and two from the rear. Pluteus turned to those in the rear and cast a new spell he recently learned - Fireball. The seven-foot mushroom man formed a ball of flame in his hands, swirling round and round. He thrust his hands forward, similar to how he throws his Ice Spike, and the flaming ball sped towards its target, hitting it without contest. The guard was engulfed in flames and dropped instantly to the bottom of the chamber with the others, his wings curling up and melting instantly from the sheer heat alone.

Two other guards were on Ooph's position, towering over them. They went to strike with their lances, but Minorha turned, stepping over her small Ribbet friend and taking the brunt of the damage. The other, now confronted with a much larger adversary, attempted to attack Minny. As he struck her with his lance, he hit her shell, sending vibrations along the shaft and disorientating him.

The third remaining Vespi-Fae engaged with the party, moved aggressively towards Purvan and attacked the Halfling with ease, Purvan taking a severe blow from his opponent.

The Queen, who hovered above the throne, Nectarion just below in front of her, summoned four hidden crystals that began to levitate around her. While smaller, it was obvious that these crystals were the likeness of the Omega Crystal, probably clones that had been produced by the Novum Arcanum, even more likely the ones that were stolen a couple of weeks ago by unknown assailants.

As the Queen gestured, two of the crystals moved to the foreground, and from them, powerful arcs of arcane energy shot out, hitting the ground close to Nectarion. Seeing this, the rest of the party fired up. Minny's face expressed her rage as she readied for her next attack. Pluteus, standing just behind her, turned and saw the *Mad Queen* and the crystals flying around her. Switching it up from a game of fire to ice, he formed an Ice Spike and propelled it towards the *Mad Queen*, piercing her abdomen. She staggered a moment and then regained her balance.

Still several feet from Nectarion, Minny continued to deal with the Vespi-Fae. In her whirlwind motion, she attacked the two currently in front of her, bludgeoning them severely. She glanced over momentarily and saw the crystals floating around the Queen, and two of them fired streams of energy, hitting Nectarion. Becoming anxious as she saw her friend in trouble, she wished to be at his side.

From between Minorha's legs, Oophaga came forth with her broadsword and in a ballet of frog-like moves, they ran their sword through the first one in front of Minny and then, before the blood on the sword could even hit the ground, they had run the second one through as well, both falling to the bottom with their fellow slain.

Pluteus, standing next to Purvan, went to his comrade's aid, and his hands gestured in a swirling motion. A transparent force gathered in his palms as an intense gravitational sphere was formed, and he cast Power Push. The force hit the last of the Vespi-Fae, sending him flying across the chamber and hitting the wall, the force so intense that it crushed the guard and cracked the side of the wall. Broken and limp, its body fell, just as the others had. Finally, Pluteus moved over to Minny and cast Tava's Armour. A blue shimmer of arcane power covered Minny, reinforcing her hard, turtle shell.

Purvan turned to view the scenario his friend was involved in, Nectarion and the *Mad Queen*. Before him, he waved his hands and warped the space in front of him, opening an Arcane Door. Its partner, opening off to the side of the Queen. As she noticed this, Purvan sent through an Arcane Barrage, hitting the Queen. Small explosions surrounded her as the impact of magical projectiles

211

found their mark. She looked over at Purvan with a sneer of detest and smugness.

With the Vespi-Fae dispatched, Minny ran towards Nectarion's position, jumping the ten-foot gap between the platform and the throne, and landed with a thud, the ground beneath showing signs of impact.

The party began to show signs of exhaustion. Minny had taken many blows defending her companions, Purvan had taken a severe hit, and Nectarion was at the forefront with the Queen. He loosened the grip on his axe ever so slightly and swung it up towards her, striking her hard. It continued and curved back around for a second blow before returning to him. She herself was beginning to wear down, but she wasn't done yet.

Closing the gap between her and Necatrion now, she swung her sceptre at him like a staff, wounding him. Then two more crystals fired arcs of energy at him. The attack left him struggling to maintain his stance as he slipped a little. She then turned to Minny and attacked her with the sceptre as well, with another two arcs of arcane power coming from the crystals and hitting her.

The Queen, showing her prowess and power, was grinding them down. She looked down on Nectarion, as if he were some filthy, disease-ridden peasant, a grin of satisfaction on her face.

"I was here when they found my sister's body, lying right where you are. I almost couldn't contain myself. Her pathetic, lifeless body. I wanted to celebrate."

Hearing this, Nectarion looked up, injuries all over and wounds bleeding, Minny standing by his side, exhausted. He could hear a slight echo, the voice of his former queen, Aurianna. He looked at the skull of Aurianna that he had been carrying through all his journey, the memories he had of her, serving her, and a slight drop of a tear welled in the corner of one of his eyes.

He mustered all he had left, the vibration of his wings reaching new speeds. Anger and rage filled his very being, and he leapt up off the ground twenty feet into the air, his axe poised for striking, in a criss-cross attack. Nectarion sliced through the *Mad Queen* as if she were buttered honey, separating her into four pieces that slowly separated from each other and hit the floor as she reached her end. The four crystals fell from the air and shattered, hundreds of tiny crystal shards scattered across the ground.

Nectarion hovered back down slowly and fell to the ground himself, on his knees, gasping for breath in exhaustion. Minny stepped up to him and placed a hand on his shoulder; she was too battered and beaten. The others, still on the other side of the gap, look on in relief that their friends are okay and that it is over.

Nectarion moved towards the pieces of the *Mad Queen* and placed the skull of her sister next to her, reciting a prayer to his goddess Apithara. A moment of reflection as he processed the situation. His mission complete, his queen avenged, his pain released.

Chapter Fifteen

Several weeks had passed by since the defeat of the *Mad Queen*, Espiritte. Mellivara had reclaimed her throne and commanded the Apis-Military to stand down and return home. Unfortunately, while the party had been dispatching Espiritte, the Apis-Military had marched on Goshan, and Lord Obo had refused to surrender. When the military had returned to the hive, a full report was given to the Queen by the commanding officers of the assault.

The troops entered the city and began to arrest the citizens, only to be met with resistance as they fought back. They were no match for the elite soldiers of the Apis-Fae, unfortunately, and many were gravely injured or killed.

Many structures were damaged or destroyed. Houses were damaged, and major buildings were set alight.

Final reports indicate that fifty percent of the population was lost in the conflict.

The party had remained in Aurisolis to assist with Mellivara's reinstatement and to apprehend any additional enemies still within the hive. Mellivara then charged the party with interrogating the Vespi-Fae prisoners to discover the full extent of her aunt's scheme.

Stellda had predicted right, it was Espirittte that was responsible for the theft of the crystals she had used in battle. The

Vespi-Fae, with their exceptional skills in subterfuge, managed to enter the Hall of Mages and retrieve them. It was also discovered that she had sought the prime Omega Crystal, hiring a thief to obtain it, only to be thwarted and killed in the attempt.

By now, reports from Goshan had made it to the hive. While most matched the Apis-Military's, a few additional details had come to light.

The civilians were attacked by the Apis-Fae; many fell in the battle, and others fled or hid. Once the outer city had been evacuated, the Apis-Military turned towards the inner city. The few remaining city guards, under the command of Commander Samuel Tombo and the Mages of Goshan, defended the Great Keep to the best of their ability. Many of them fell in battle. Just as the Apis-Fae were about to breach the Great Keep, they halted. They simply stopped and turned, leaving the city without a word.

A list accompanied the report of those who had fallen in the battle, including Commander Samual Tombo and Siriana Mastiri, a silver mage of the Novum Arcanum.

Queen Mellivara expressed her deepest sorrows at this news and felt an extreme amount of responsibility for the actions of her people. She sent word back to Lord Obo in Gosahn that if he and his people would allow it, she would do all she could to assist in the rebuilding of the city and, most importantly, the relations between the two peoples. She reiterated that Aurisolis would continue to do its duty in the pollination of the Orchard Forest regardless of the decision.

After remaining in Aurisolis for a week, the Queen held a light-hearted celebration and a ceremony, honouring the party for its deeds in restoring her to the throne. Nectarion was awarded the highest honour for completing his mission and offered the position of Queen's King, a position that had not been filled in many centuries. If he takes the posting, it will require him to remain in Aurisolis by his Queen's side.

The following day, the companions decided to return to Goshan and offer their assistance there. As they entered the city, they could see the damage that it had incurred. Houses reduced to rubble, and while the fires no longer burned, the charred remains of them could still be seen.

Going before Lord Obo, he expressed his eternal gratitude for the party's valiant efforts. While sorrow hung heavily on him, he was grateful that he and the remaining citizens were still alive. Nectarion presented him with his Queen's offer to aid them, to which he said he would address the situation at a later date.

By the middle of Jun, the colder days had set in. The Lord Governor and the citizens of Goshan held a ceremony of their own to honour the party and a memorial service to those who had lost their lives in the battle. The Lady Athalia of Westhold and Lord Governor Tedia Barak of Prokk attended with many other dignitaries, including Daten, Raspen and Lakku from the Fractured Anvil. A monument was commissioned by Lord Obo to be erected in the market square outside the inner city gate as a remembrance.

The end of the month approached, and the Winter Festival was but a few days away. Lord Obo used what resources he had to provide the people with a respite from the depressing current

216

events. The party did their best to help, of course, but by the day of the festival's start, the mood that covered the city was glum at best. The denizens had little need to feel cheer or celebration, as much was lost. Family and friends, neighbours and community figures.

On the second day of the festival, the markets opened for the morning and then closed. In the evening, the civilians gathered outside the Great Keep and lit candles, sang songs and gave thanks for their survival and prayers for their lost ones. Many townsfolk gifted each other with essential items that they may have needed: blankets, clothing and food.

The group had decided to meet at Purvan's penthouse for dinner that night. The past weeks had been hectic with ceremonies and offers of positions to higher standing. They felt that they had not actually had time to breathe and just be casual, as they had often done since their meeting.

The party, in such a short time, had become close and formed a strong bond. They had almost become like a family.

After everyone had arrived, it was noticed that Oophaga was not in attendance, to which Purvan said he would explain after dinner.

The table was full of food, chicken, and a large turkey sat in the centre surrounded by cheese, bread, vegetables, mashed potatoes, corn, peas and a big plate of something new called fish fingers. Bottles of wine, jugs of mead and spiced rum rested between the dishes, and the companions sat down to their quiet but substantial meal.

As the hours of the evening rolled by, most of the food had been consumed. Pluteus, at one end of the table, with the bowl of peas all to himself. His mouth was full when he asked the question.

"So, where is Ooph? You said you would tell us."

Purvan retrieved a piece of parchment and unrolled it.

Dear friends, I have experienced much in such a short time, more than I ever believed I would. I have come to think of you as my family, and the support you have shown me can not be measured. But the wild calls me, and there are things that I still need to discover. Not so much about the world but more so, myself.

Do not fret for me, for I know my journey will lead me back to you all. Whatever path lies before you, I hope you find what it is you seek.

Your friend, Oophaga.

"They left?" said Pluteus, stunned momentarily.

A silence fell on the room when Nectarion broke it with an announcement.

"My friends, I too have come to care for you all, and as Oophaga mentioned, you are like a family. But as you are aware, Queen Mellivara has offered me an important position within the hive, and I feel within me the need to return home."

"You're leaving too?" Minny questioned in dismay.

"I am afraid so. But please don't think this is the end of our friendship, I expect you to come and visit, and I, too, will visit you."

Tears began to well in Minny's eyes. It had been some time since she had a real bond with anyone, and now that she did, she felt like it was all falling apart.

"Is anyone else thinking of leaving?" she asked, voice shaking.

Looking at her, Purvan reluctantly chimed in.

"Lord Obo has offered me the posting of diplomatic attaché to the Fractured Anvil. If I accept, I will be a key member of an envoy to open full relations between our two peoples. The envoy leaves in two weeks."

"Well, I'm not going anywhere." Pluteus blurted out.

The room had lost any spirit it had contained when they first arrived.

Purvan stood up and took his goblet in hand.

"I understand you are upset at this news, these partings. But I have lived for many decades and seen friends and rivals come and go. It is these people who come into our lives and even leave that shape us to be who we are. As a *student of life,* I know for a fact that there are many paths to tread and if we part and are meant to reunite, then we will."

The faces of his guests remained in a sorrowful state.

"I want you to remember the good times we have had, the dangers we have faced and cherish all those moments, because they may never come again. After all, we are only mortal."

He raised his goblet.

"To friends. To family," He drank. The others begrudgingly followed suit.

Just as he concluded his toast, the party could hear a sweet melody rising from outside. They moved to the window and looked out onto the square in front of the Great Keep. There, they saw the townspeople, lit candles in their hands, singing.

> *"Lean on me, when you're not strong*
> *And I'll be your friend*
> *I'll help you carry on."*

"Do you know this one, Purvan?" Nectarion asked.

With a cheeky grin, Purvan opened the window and picked up the tune on the next line, as did the others.

> *"For it won't be long*
> *'Til I'm gonna need*
> *Somebody to lean on…"*

******

As the scene ends on this moment of sorrow, cheer and melancholy, it pulls back, revealing the square full of townspeople, the Great Keep, Goshan, the east coast, and finally all of Edron, continuing on into the sky as we end on a small bluish-green world, somewhere in the Cosmos.

Epilogue

Westhold:

The Lady Athalia stood near her desk, looking out the large window towards the west. The treeline of the Redwood Forest sat on the horizon as the sun slowly descended into its slumber. A city guard entered the room and stopped just short of the desk.

"My Lady, the first reports from our scouts on the far side of Redwood have come in. They don't sound promising, I'm afraid."

"Thank you, Captain. Proceed."

"The territory referred to as Tarin Marr seems to be amassing a force. The small villages close to the edge of the forest have substantial troop numbers."

The Lady's face turned stoic.

"Continue."

"Also, we have information picked up by our contacts in the Underground. It seems that the ruler of this kingdom is quite a fanatical and xenophobic."

"Anything else, Captain?" she asked casually.

"No, my Lady."

"Thank you, Captain. Return to your post and inform me of anything that comes to your attention."

The captain remained for a moment, expecting something else before acknowledging the command.

"Yes, my Lady."

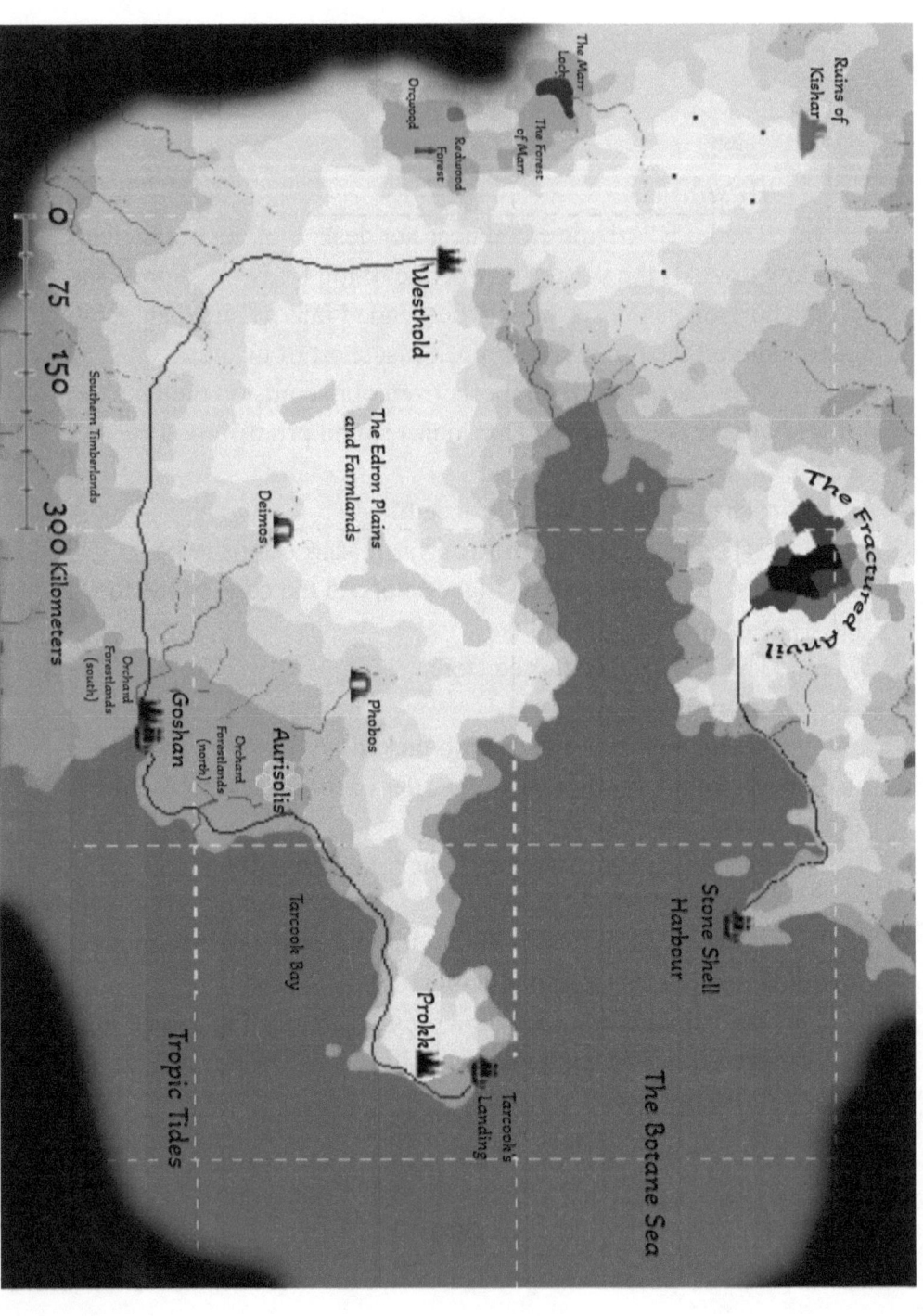

Glossary

Apis-Fae - A subspecies of Faerie folk that resembles anthropomorphic bees. With two legs, four arms and wings.

Drakona - Resemble wingless dragons in humanoid form and possess a powerful elemental breath.

Faeries - Are winged humanoid creatures with insectile features.

Fungril - Resemble humanoid mushrooms.

Galapa - Resemble anthropomorphic turtles with large, domed shells into which they can retract into.

Ribbet - Ribbets resemble anthropomorphic frogs with protruding eyes and webbed hands and feet.

Tuden - Tudor, an architectural and design movement combining English Perpendicular Gothic and Northern Renaissance elements, characterised by decorative half-timbering, steeply pitched roofs with multiple gables, large groups of windows, and prominent chimneys.

Vespi-Fae - A subspecies of Faerie folk that resembles anthropomorphic wasps. With two legs, four arms and wings.

www.ingramcontent.com/pod-product-compliance
Lightning Source LLC
Chambersburg PA
CBHW020513120726
47904CB00003B/809